Sjón

Born in Reykjavík in 1962, Sjón is the author of the novels *The Blue Fox, The Whispering Muse, From the Mouth of the Whale, Moonstone* and *CoDex 1962*, for which he has won several awards including the Nordic Council's Literature Prize and the Icelandic Literary Prize. He has also been shortlisted for the International IMPAC Dublin Literary Award and the *Independent* Foreign Fiction Prize, and his work has been translated into thirty-five languages.

In addition, Sjón has written nine poetry collections as well as four opera librettos and lyrics for various artists. He lives in Reykjavík, Iceland.

Victoria Cribb has translated over thirty-five books by Icelandic authors. Her translations of *Moonstone* and *CoDex 1962* were both longlisted for the PEN America Translation Prize and she received the Ord–stír honorary translation award for services to Icelandic literature in 2017.

RED MILK

SJÓN

Translated from the Icelandic by
Victoria Cribb

SCEPTRE

Originally published in Icelandic in 2019 by JPV Publishing,
Iceland, as *Korngult hár, grá augu*
First published in Great Britain in 2021 by Sceptre
An imprint of Hodder & Stoughton
An Hachette UK company

This paperback edition published in 2022

1

This book has been translated with financial support from
🛡 ICELANDIC LITERATURE CENTER

A CIP catalogue record for this title is available from the British Library

Paperback ISBN 9781529355925
eBook ISBN 9781529355901

Typeset in Sabon MT by Palimpsest Book Production Ltd,
Falkirk, Stirlingshire

Printed and bound in Great Britain by Clays Ltd, Elcograf S.p.A.

Hodder & Stoughton policy is to use papers that are natural, renewable
and recyclable products and made from wood grown in sustainable forests.
The logging and manufacturing processes are expected to conform to the
environmental regulations of the country of origin.

Hodder & Stoughton Ltd
Carmelite House
50 Victoria Embankment
London EC4Y 0DZ

www.sceptrebooks.co.uk

I

Of three metamorphoses of the spirit I tell you: how the spirit becomes a camel; and the camel, a lion; and the lion, finally, a child.

Friedrich Nietzsche, *Thus Spoke Zarathustra*

i

Mist has formed on the cool glass where cheek and mouth touch the window. Seen from the compartment door, the man's reflection blends into the railway station outside: the entrance to the platform, the clock on the brick wall beside it and the canopy protecting passengers from the hot August sun. It is thirteen minutes past one and, according to the ticket lying on the seat beside the man, it was here at Cheltenham Spa that his journey from Paddington was supposed to end. The train arrived punctually – at twelve forty-four – but it has been sitting at the platform for nearly half an hour now, and the passenger in the overcoat has reached his journey's end in more senses than one. Yet from the mist on the window it is evident that he has not been dead for long – although his head is cooling fast, it still retains a lingering warmth.

There are two policemen in the railway compartment. One is busy going through the outside pockets of the man's coat, where he discovers half a bar of chocolate, three small balls of scrunched-up wrapper and silver foil, a key on a simple ring and a London Transport bus ticket. He unbuttons the dead man's coat, revealing that underneath he is wearing a pair of blue-striped pyjamas embroidered with the name of a West London hospital.

The inside pockets yield a recent passport with a photo of the man, issued in Reykjavík, Iceland, stating that he is twenty-four years old and his name is Gunnar Pálsson Kampen; a wallet containing Icelandic krónur and British pound notes; a thick envelope of money bearing the logo of a respected English private bank; and a folded sheet of paper with written instructions on how to travel by bus from Cheltenham Spa Station to the village of Guiting Power and a sketch map of the footpath from there to Pinnock Cliffs. Beside this last name someone has drawn a cross that has been converted into a swastika by the addition of four red lines. There is a red biro in the breast pocket of the man's pyjama jacket.

The other policeman is holding a notebook. In it, he writes in pencil: *'Blond hair, grey eyes'*, below which he produces a deft sketch of the body and the railway compartment.

The policeman who has finished going through the dead man's pockets turns to his colleague and shakes his head. They both look out of the carriage window. A small crowd has gathered on the platform to watch what is happening inside the compartment. Neither officer notices the three men in black shirts hurrying away from the train and disappearing into the station building.

ii

Had he been old enough to understand the word he heard from his mother's lips at the beginning of that day – the word that later on would provide his first conscious memories of himself?

He had tried to mimic it but could hear that he had failed. He knew what water was, and he knew the names of all the colours and recognised one of them in what she had said, but the combination was new and so could mean something quite different.

His mother had twisted round in the front seat, leant towards him and repeated the word, very slowly, breaking it up into four parts. Her red-painted lips moved with each part as she summoned the sounds from her mind with the aid of her tongue, facial muscles, mouth cavity, throat and the air from her lungs, forming an open spout to release the 'R' that her tongue had formed by vibrating against the roof of her mouth just behind her small front teeth, then clearing the way for the 'au' by dropping her tongue to the teeth of her lower jaw, and, in the space between, poking out its wet tip and vibrating it even faster as she blew out the 'th', then whipping it back inside her mouth to produce the 'a' which was still reverberating when she raised her lower lip to the edge of her front teeth, vibrating there in the 'v', which vanished as her mouth opened up for another 'a', then closed in a brief 't', her tongue shooting so quickly to the roof of her mouth that he could barely glimpse it before she blew out the final 'n' through her delicate nostrils.

'Rau-da-va-tn. We're going to Raudavatn.'

Redwater.

The driver's door was wrenched open. His father got behind the wheel, started the engine and off they went. His mother turned round to face the front. He tucked his legs underneath him on the back seat, sensing that his father was watching him in the rear-view mirror.

His two sisters had sat him down between them. It was their job to make sure he didn't stand up on the seat, but when he did so anyway, neither lifted a finger to stop him. Through the rear windscreen he watched their house growing smaller as the car drew away. His stomach tightened with fear. In no time at all, their house was so small that he would never fit back inside. It was then that he remembered the fly.

In the right-hand pocket of his shorts was a matchbox. And inside the matchbox was a bluebottle, a gift from the big boy who lived in the basement of the three-storey house down the road. The boy had been hanging around with him and his sisters on the pavement in front of the house while they waited for their parents. As the June sun warmed the wall, the white cladding, salty from the winter's sea-laden winds, had attracted the newly woken flies. Black as pitch, they buzzed their song and took it in turns to alight on the wall, where they would perch for an instant, silent but fidgeting, only to take off again if you tried to catch them. Though these lady flies were as fat as his thumb, it was hard to grab hold of them. The big boy, noticing what he was trying to do, had pulled three matchboxes out of his pocket. Selecting a red-and-white one, he had half opened it to demonstrate to Gunnar and his sisters that it was empty. Then, after motioning them to stand back from the wall, he had clapped the box, quick as a flash, over one of the bluebottles and snapped it shut.

They had taken it in turns to hold the matchbox, which vibrated excitingly in their hands with the bluebottle's frantic bumbling. They'd held it up to their ears, listening to the fly as it buzzed and tried to take flight in the darkness, battering against the sides with bumps and drones. But the moment their mother came out of the house and waved to the sisters to get in the car, the big boy had taken himself off, after first slipping the matchbox into the pocket of Gunnar's shorts. A few moments later, Gunnar too was in the car.

Now he was standing on the back seat, watching their house dwindle to nothing as they turned out of the street. The pang of fear had gone. The fly buzzed in his pocket.

'Make your brother sit down!'

Their father spoke sharply. His sisters dragged him down and forced him to face the front, pinning him there, each with a hand on one of his skinny thighs. When he tried to wriggle out of their grasp, they tightened their grip with silent determination. One of the sisters remarked to the other:

'It's like I can still hear that fly.'

In the front, their mother began to sing a variation on 'Ása's Ballad', tapping a finger in time on the tip of her husband's nose.

> *Ása walked the streets with dignity.*
> *She heard a fair commotion by Salófí.*
> *Hihanna ho! Sing-a-ling pump!*
> *Kansilorum kantatorum pumpi.*

'Raudavatn.'

Redwater.

Halfway between the west end of Reykjavík and their destination, this unintelligible word finally conjured up a picture in his mind:

A glass, brimming with red milk.

When they got there, the water turned out not to be red at all, except right under the banks where you could see down to the rust-coloured gravel of the lake bed. He scooped up a handful, which trickled away between his fingers, as limpid as the water in the laundry tub he had his baths in at home. But you could skim stones on it. And although his own pebbles plopped straight into the water, he was party to the miracle of making flat stones bounce over the smooth surface.

On the way home he let the fly loose in the car.

iii

The year Gunnar Pálsson Kampen was born, his father created a den for himself in a windowless cubbyhole off the marital bedroom. He furnished it with a small desk and stool, a single bookshelf and a floor lamp with two bulbs: one red, one white. On the desk was a shortwave radio and a wooden-framed photograph of himself with his brother and sister, while the walls were hung with two maps – one of the world, the other of Europe – and a calendar issued by his employer, the Icelandic Steamship Company. Two wires extended from the radio: one an electrical cable that was plugged into an adapter along with the lamp, the other an aerial that ran up the unpainted partition wall to disappear through a hole in the wood. About halfway between the map of the world and the aerial cable hung a bundle of birch twigs, lashed together with coarse string.

Throughout the Second World War, up to Churchill's Iron Curtain speech and beyond, Páll Kampen spent most of his nights closeted in his den, listening to the news – not just in languages he knew well like his Norwegian mother tongue, English and German, but in French, which he was gaining an ever better understanding of, and also in some languages that were completely alien to him. In the latter cases he tried to deduce from the announcers' tones how the war was affecting the various nations, such as Japan, Turkey and Greece. When his wife Erla went to bed, he would remove the white light bulb, screw in the red one, and don the headphones he had acquired at work, to allow him to continue listening without, as he put it, being in anyone's way.

What he couldn't hear were the involuntary cries and groans, the bangings on the table and stampings on the floor that the news provoked, which kept his family awake. But no one ever mentioned this.

Of all the objects in the den, it was the bundle of twigs that held Gunnar's undivided attention once he had begun to take an interest in the world around him. With this birch, his father had been beaten by his own father; often, according to him, for some minor misdemeanour, though he never went into details. As Gunnar couldn't imagine his father as a little boy, his mind conjured up scenes of a titanic struggle between Páll and the grandfather Gunnar had never known. There were no photographs of Harald Edvard Kampen, who had died in another country before Gunnar was born, so Gunnar pictured him as an older, larger, more fearsome version of his father, who seemed to him quite large enough as it was.

In the imagined scenes, this white-haired ancient lunged at his grown-up son with a huge, outstretched hand, bellowing at him that he shouldn't have done this or that bad thing – invariably something he couldn't possibly have known he must or mustn't do, something trivial, that in no way justified the old man's violence – and snatched with his long, crooked fingers until he caught him. Then a dreadful struggle would ensue, in which father and son fought like wild animals. At first they were evenly matched (the model for Gunnar's imagined spectacle was the illustration of a battle between a wolf and a grizzly bear in an American book for boys), but it inevitably ended with Páll Kampen dangling, limp as a dead cat, in his father's grasp. The grandfather always fought with one hand, brandishing the birch in the other. Once he had got Gunnar's father by the scruff of the neck, he would force 'the boy' to his knees, bending him right over until his forehead touched the floor, then yank down his trousers and rain blows on his buttocks and thighs.

Gunnar had once seen his father hurl his mother right across the kitchen. It was easy to imagine a similar difference in strength. Every time the action film of the fight between his father and grandfather played out in Gunnar's mind, he felt a little more affectionate towards his father than he had before.

'It doesn't matter any more what it was used for.'

Páll Kampen, clerk in the Steamship Company stockroom, ran his fingers slowly over the birch, which responded to his touch with a quiet crackling. It was so dry and brittle that the twigs would have snapped at the first blow, but Gunnar wasn't to know this. Páll continued, with a catch in his voice:

'The main thing is that it's here with me.'

The birch was all Páll had to remember his father by, and now that death has freed the grandson's body from its incurable disease and Gunnar is slumped lifeless on a seat in a train compartment in a siding at Cheltenham Spa Station, the memory of the birch, the den and his father is second in the series of memories that flashes in front of his mind's eye before disappearing from him and the world for good. Silence reigns in his chest – but his brain is still working.

Even as the imprint of the birch is fading, it snatches another memory along with it.

Gunnar was lying in his parents' big bed with his mother and his two elder sisters, Astrid and Sólveig. Something had happened to make Erla want the children to sleep with her that night. He was five years old. No one told him what had happened and he didn't ask, because camping in his parents' bed like that was quite exciting enough.

It was dark in the room. The light from the den forced its way out around the door, like a fiery red frame on the darkened wall. From behind the closed door came the sound of muffled sobbing. Gunnar turned his head on the pillow to see if Sólveig, lying next to him, was awake too. When he saw the gleam of his sister's eyes, he wriggled closer to her and whispered:

'Daddy's looking at the birch.'

She hissed back: 'No, you idiot; Daddy's frightened of Hitler.'

iv

The Sleipnir Cycling Club was based in a large garage on Hofsvallagata, the neighbouring road to Mánavallagata, where the Kampen family home stood, in the west end of town. The two streets ran parallel, their houses back to back, their gardens forming a large, enclosed play area which was safe even for toddlers. Mothers could send their young children out of the back door and be sure of finding them again, if not in their own garden, then in the patch belonging to next door or next-door-but-one. Gunnar was one of these children.

The cycling club garage, which projected at an angle into the garden area behind Erla and Páll Kampen's house, exuded a sweet smell of bicycle oil. At weekends it was presided over by a man in his thirties called Lúther Alfredsson, the club chairman, who also smelt of oil. In fine weather, he would open the garage doors on the garden side and wheel out whichever bicycle he happened to be repairing at the time. He would turn it upside down and balance it on its saddle and handlebars while he patched or replaced the inner tubes, or lubricated the axles and chain. Members of the

Sleipnir Club often kept him company as they overhauled their bikes before embarking on a group outing along Reykjavík's northern shore or out to Seltjarnarnes at the westernmost tip of the peninsula. But they were more than just fair-weather cyclists. In pouring rain they sported ankle-length waterproof capes that covered both man and bicycle, flapping around them like the outspread wings of a great black-backed gull. Once everyone's vehicle was roadworthy, Lúther would give them the sign – a quick blast on the railway guard's whistle acquired on his solo trip through German-speaking Europe in the summer of 1937 – and before turning their bicycles the right way up the members would all spin their pedals in unison with their hands, faster and faster, until the silvery rear wheels began to hum, to the delight of the crowd of children who had gathered on the patch of grass by the garage expressly to watch this spectacle. Then Lúther would give another blast on his whistle, and the members of Sleipnir would grab their bicycles, swing them upright, mount their saddles and speed away, to a shrill chorus of bells. Once beyond the outskirts of the town they would begin conversing in German, since, in addition to being an organisation dedicated to cycling and a healthy way of life, Sleipnir, under Lúther's leadership, acted as a German language school.

Gunnar was intrigued by what went on in the cycle shed. The first thing he did when his mother sent him out to play was to see if Lúther was there. He would toddle out of his garden, across the gravel path that formed a notional division between Mánavallagata and the next street, and onto the patch of grass in front of the garage. There he would knock on the door and call out Lúther's name.

'Loo-de, Loo-de . . . !'

Sometimes the door would open and Lúther, dressed in his brown overalls, would stick out his head, giving off that sweet whiff of oil and holding in his hand some tool or a part that he was repairing. But not every day. The chairman of the cycling club was a senior teacher at a secondary school in the east end of town, a half-hour cycle ride away. By the time Lúther came home from work it was generally Gunnar's teatime and Gunnar was too young to be allowed out after that.

Later – but not much later – Gunnar discovered that he could reach the handle of the garage door. It turned out to be unlocked.

Inside the empty shed a shadowy silence prevailed, of the kind that often impinges on one's consciousness in places that normally house noisy activity or equipment. The gleaming black bicycles stood in a double row along one wall, facing into the middle: a silent promise of speed, hissing tyres and tinkling bells. Against the wall opposite them were the work benches, the lathe, and shelves of spare parts, large and small.

Gunnar stubbed his toe on some object that was lying on the floor. Bending down, he saw that he had kicked over a stack of round metal plates. He picked one up and turned it over. There was a picture on the front. He held it up to the faint shaft of light that entered by the narrow window above the lathe. The picture consisted of a red cross with eight arms, four of them broader than the others, on a white background, enclosed by a blue circle; it was a cross, sun or wheel, the old badge of the Sleipnir Cycling Club, which used to adorn the members' bikes, screwed on to the head tube below the lamp, but had been abandoned shortly after the arrival of the British army of occupation, a little less than two years earlier. Gunnar dropped the badge; he had spied something more interesting.

Hanging from the ceiling were two child's bicycles and one tricycle.

Next time Lúther appeared in the garden, Erla came over for a word. She asked if it was true, as she had heard, that he had child's bicycles for sale. Not that he was aware of, he said. At this point Gunnar stepped in front of his mother and marched into the garage. Erla and Lúther followed him inside and when all three re-emerged, Gunnar was the proud owner of the tricycle.

Lúther stroked Gunnar's blond head:

'You can join the club once you've practised enough.'

Gunnar pedalled off down the gravel path.

Erla folded her arms:

'We'll see what Páll has to say about that.'

Lúther pointed to the Kampens' garden:

'You can pay me in spuds. Twelve should do.'

V

Kirsten Sigrid Kampen came to stay exactly two months after peace had been declared and the Germans and Quislings had surrendered in Norway. The family went down to the harbour to meet her, and the instant she appeared on deck Gunnar recognised his aunt from the photo in the radio den of his father with his brother and sister. He nudged Sólveig and pointed to a thin woman who now began to pick her way unsteadily down the gangplank, clinging to the rail, moving slowly, descending step by cautious step towards the dock. Her head was covered by a scarf and on top of this a hat cast a shadow over her pale face, which was already half hidden by round sunglasses, while the rest of her was encased in a close-fitting brown woollen coat and a black skirt, and in her hand she carried a small suitcase.

Sólveig shook her head: no, this timid figure, dressed for a nippy evening in October rather than a brilliantly sunny day in July, couldn't possibly be the jolly Norwegian aunt her father had told them so many stories about.

'Without her we'd have died of grief when the cancer took our mother. But Kirsten could play a tune on a blade of grass, and not only that but she could dance to the tune she played. It was a pretty dance.'

Whenever Páll reminisced about his sister, a quick movement would ripple through his body, like a twitch passing from his right shoulder to his left. As this twitch, induced by a quivering blade of grass when he was small like them, was the closest the children had ever seen their father come to dancing, they were convinced that their aunt must be the jolliest person on earth. This belief was only enhanced by the fact that the letters and postcards she wrote to her brother were signed 'KiKi'. To the sisters, Astrid and Sólveig, this was the height of sophistication.

Hard on the heels of the faltering woman, who Gunnar insisted was their aunt, came a young man. He peered impatiently past her, and although it didn't occur to him, any more than it had to any of the other passengers who had descended ahead of him, to offer her a hand, he did at least manage to refrain from pushing past until they had reached the bottom of the gangplank. At that point, he shoved her aside with such force that the sunglasses fell off Kirsten Kampen's face and she stumbled forwards, dropping the suitcase, which landed on the dock with a crash and burst open. The young man, striding over to meet his family, didn't so much as glance over his shoulder.

After a first, instinctive look around for help, the woman seemed to recollect herself and set about picking up the small heap of clothes, underwear and other personal items that lay scattered for all to see, along with a man's black suit. The few onlookers who noticed her made no attempt to come to her aid and her hurried movements suggested that she hadn't been expecting them to either.

Páll was still scanning the crowd for his sister when Gunnar ran over to the woman who was kneeling beside her suitcase. He stooped to pick up her sunglasses and handed them to her. She took them and put them on. Once they were in place, she found herself confronted by the outstretched hand of her brother Páll, who had followed the boy to prevent him from falling into the harbour between the ship and the dock. To the puzzlement of the children, no word passed between brother and sister, no dancing twitch rippled through their father's shoulders. He shook his head unobtrusively and she lowered her eyes.

Páll helped Kirsten to her feet, took her by the arm and led her away. Astrid and Sólveig ordered Gunnar to come with them. When he asked them why their father hadn't hugged his sister, they replied that it was like that when people hadn't seen each other for a long time; if they touched, they would only break down in tears. They would put off that sort of display until they got home. He ought to know that it was bad manners to cry in front of strangers.

At home on Mánavallagata, there was more shouting than weeping. Although Kirsten and Páll did shed a few tears in between yelling at each other behind closed doors in the sitting room, in practice it was Erla who did most of the crying, as the children, eavesdropping from upstairs, overheard. Their mother had burst into tears the moment she set eyes on her sister-in-law, cried even harder after flinging her arms around her, and when Kirsten had taken off her hat and scarf, Erla's crying had turned into a wail.

In the photo of the Kampen siblings – Páll, Hjort Helge and KiKi – which the children had so often studied, their aunt was a young girl with long, blonde locks. These had disappeared.

Kirsten Kampen stayed with her brother for over a year, which was how long it took her to recover from whatever had been ailing her and stripped her of all her hair. She slept in the spare room but, since she found it hard to be alone, a camp bed was made up for Gunnar and put in there with her. Every morning, or whenever she remembered, she handed a measuring tape to her small roommate so that he could measure how much her hair had grown in the night. She said it would grow faster if someone else was waiting for it with her. When it grew back, it was grey.

She never went out among the townspeople – not even with Páll to the National Day coffee party held by Nordmannslaget, the Norwegian association in Iceland, of which he was president – but she always accepted invitations to accompany the family on excursions out of town. On these outings she would sometimes blow a tune on a blade of grass so the children could dance.

By the end of August 1946, her hair reached down to her shoulders. She was better. Erla helped her to tint it and set it in a cold perm to bring the curls along.

One mild autumn afternoon, Gunnar came home from school to discover that she had left the country. On his camp bed lay the black suit, with best wishes from his Aunt KiKi.

vi

'You come, boy.'

The voice carries to him with the orange glow of a floor lamp, which stands next to an armchair by a wall lined from floor to ceiling with books. It is evening. Gunnar is poised in the opening where the dining room is partitioned off from the library by a set of sliding double doors, the two halves of which are partially closed, leaving just enough room for a narrow-shouldered nine-year-old to slip through. His parents are with their hosts and other guests in the smart drawing room, from which a babble of voices and the odd burst of laughter reach his ears. The party is livening up, the volume of the adults' voices is rising; any minute now they'll break into song. He meanwhile had decided to do a little exploring. He brings with him a waft of food, cigars and alcohol, as he senses now in the chill wintry air that breathes towards him from the dimly lit library. There's a window open in there.

The source of the voice, which had delivered these words in broken Icelandic, proves to be a human figure, sitting in the shadow thrown by the curved back of the armchair.

Instead of answering, Gunnar moves his right foot into reverse, as stealthily as he can. His big toe presses down into the thick carpet, followed by the ball of his foot, then he leans carefully backwards and begins to shift his weight from left foot to right, without losing his balance. Since the birth of his younger brother, he has become adept at creeping around on tiptoe. It is because of his brother that Gunnar is here this evening: he didn't want to be left at home with his sisters to babysit Hördur. And as this is the first time since the birth that his mother has come out to meet people, she decided it would be fun to bring Gunnar along. Páll Kampen resignedly agreed and so the three of them had attended the fundraising concert by the Reykjavík Mixed Voice Choir at the Idnó Theatre, followed by a reception at the home of the director. Erla was planning to start going to choir practice again in the new year.

The voice issuing from the armchair prods at Gunnar. He wobbles.

'Not to fear, not to fear me.'

A hand is extended into the corona of light under the lampshade; thin-boned, with a silver ring on the middle finger. Bracelets jangle at the wrist. The fingers seize the switch on the lamp cord and press it briskly, increasing the illumination by half, enough to reveal the person sitting in the chair. It is a woman, with features that are finely drawn but severe: small bottle-brown eyes under pencilled brows, and a sharp, not overly long, nose. She is staring straight ahead rather than at the arm that she has dispatched to perform its task like an errand boy who can be trusted to carry out his orders without supervision, and her mouth is curved in a studied smile.

Gunnar, meeting her gaze, turns red.

'No, no, never to be sorry.'

She holds out her hands in an invitation for him to join her in the library. Gunnar shoots a glance over his shoulder. Someone has pushed ajar the door between the dining room and the smart drawing room. The choirmaster appears briefly. There is clapping. A note sounds on the piano, followed by the first bars of Robert Schumann's 'Zigeunerleben'.

There is a lot that is exotic about the woman in the armchair, as he sees ever more clearly the closer he gets. She is wearing a dress made of a shiny purple fabric, with a blue-and-white shawl of the same material pinned to her left shoulder with a large brooch. Between her eyebrows is a dark-red mark the size of a small coin. He has only ever seen a woman like that in a picture book of oriental fairy tales.

'You come.'

Gunnar can't work out her accent. It doesn't sound Scandinavian or German, accents he is familiar with from his father and his father's friends, and from some of his mother's fellow singers in the mixed choir. A number of immigrants have found a home in the choir, as singing is more forgiving of deviations in language than speaking: the locals make the best fist they can of the foreign lieder and oratorios, while the immigrants' pronunciation of Icelandic is corrected by the melody of the traditional songs.

When Gunnar is close enough, the woman leans forward in her chair and takes hold of his hands. Her grip is firm and hot, and before he can pull away she tightens it. She asks what he's called and when he tells her, she says at once that Gunnar is a fine manly name; it means 'warrior'. She knows this because she is learning Icelandic so as to be able to read the ancient sagas and poems. She herself has such a peculiar three-part name that the boy forgets it as soon as he has heard it.

'I show you?'

From her intonation he gathers that this is a question, but his upbringing has taught him that when an adult asks a question, they do not expect an answer. Without releasing her grip on his left hand, she raises his right hand and pulls it under the lampshade, holding it up to the strong bulb until the light shines red through the child's flesh, revealing the silhouettes of the bones inside.

'Only possible with such a hand.'

The woman nods at him. The filigree brooch on her shoulder gleams, exposing the pattern from which it is made: a myriad tiny swastikas that differ from the hated one only in that they stand upright rather than tilted on their side.

'Only white people let the light into themselves.'

'There you are!'

Erla is standing in the doorway. Before releasing Gunnar's hands, the woman in the armchair nods to his mother and says:

'*C'est un bon garçon, madame*. He will be man of great deeds.'

vii

Fog. Statue. Crowd.
    Genies from magic lamps.
    Shadows in long overcoats.
    A pram. A woman's voice.
    Paving stones.
    Arms at his sides.
    Smashing sounds.
    Faces.
    Blood.
    Truncheon blows.
    Gas masks.
    'Here's one!'
    The colours of the Icelandic flag.
    Stones. Clods of earth. Broken glass.
    Mirror shards. A cut.
    A smile. A closed eye.

Green metal canisters. Clouds rising to the sky.
    Echoing footsteps. A pram pushed past.
    Right cheek pressed to paving stone. Paperboy's bag lost.

A figure striding into the smoke.

Like mud.

People retching.

Black helmets. Eleven years old.

'Give him to me!'

Making for the back entrance.

Paintings on the walls. Bandages and iodine.

Distinguished-looking.

Marked by battle.

Picking up a shard of mirror. A white scar.

His ear pressed to the pavement, Gunnar listens to the crowd through the fog of gas. The fog has its origin in the green metal canisters that are lying scattered over the grass around the statue of Iceland's independence hero, Jón Sigurdsson. Tear gas billows out of slits in their lids. The clouds rise to the skies like genies from magic lamps, spreading like a glittering veil over the square to form a fog that hides the throng as they scatter with echoing footsteps.

Gunnar's eyes and nose are stinging, but through his tears he can make out the shadows of men's and women's legs, moving first this way, then that. Most are trouser-clad men, some in long coats. A child's pram is propelled past Gunnar at high speed. The narrow, hard-rubber wheels rattle over the uneven paving stones. A woman shouts: 'Treachery!'

He makes an effort to get up but can't even raise his head. He is lying face down, his right cheek crushed against the concrete paving stone, his arms at his sides. There is no sign of his bag containing copies of *Althýdubladid*, the newspaper of the Social Democratic Party.

There are yet more sounds of smashing glass from the parliament building.

A figure comes running towards Gunnar and pauses right by his face. For a moment, black rubber boots block his view of the square before the booted man strides off into the smoke.

The gas in the canister nearest to him is running out, the residue oozing from the slits like mud. There is a smear of blood on the curved metal rim. It was this that had hit Gunnar on the head when, without warning, Reykjavík's chief of police ordered tear gas to be shot indiscriminately into the crowd, at both protestors and supporters of Iceland's entry into the North Atlantic Treaty Organisation.

He hears people retching. The dull thuds of truncheons.

'Here's one!'

Gunnar is hauled to his feet by two men in black helmets and gas masks. They pause when they discover that he is no more than a child.

'Give him to me! I know him.'

The man who addresses the police is dressed in civilian clothes but has a British army helmet on his head and a handkerchief tied over his nose and mouth. On his arm he wears a ribbon in the colours of the Icelandic flag.

The man, who once gave Gunnar a bluebottle, now helps him away from Austurvöllur Square, leading him to the back entrance of the Independence Party headquarters. Inside, they have already embarked on a clean-up operation, carrying out the stones and clods of earth, sweeping up shards of glass, straightening the pictures on the walls. Gunnar's saviour sits him down at a table in a meeting room and goes in search of a bandage and iodine.

A distinguished-looking middle-aged man brings Gunnar a cup of coffee:

'So young and already marked by battle.'

The man picks up a shard of mirror from the floor to show him.

Gunnar's reflection has a wound in the middle of its forehead, just above the eyebrows. A finger-length, horizontal cut that turns up at the ends in a blood-red smile. It will fade over time into a white scar resembling a closed eye.

viii

Erla was sitting at one end of the kitchen table, silently running a fingertip over the grains of sugar on the cloth, when Sólveig suddenly remembered the black suit that Aunt KiKi had left behind. Gunnar could be confirmed in a new outfit like his school friends, after all. He ought to be big enough for the suit by now, a string bean like him. The day had been saved.

Sólveig fixed Gunnar with a look, waiting for his agreement. He shrugged. She frowned and nodded towards their mother. Gunnar met her gaze, forming a soundless 'what?', then turned to Astrid with an enquiring look. She pinched his knee under the table:

'Good idea, eh?'

Gunnar flushed:

'Yes, sure . . .'

Erla straightened up in her chair but Sólveig was on her feet before her:

'Just stay with Hördur, Mum; we'll find it.'

Hördur appeared in the kitchen doorway: seven years old in body, four years old in mind:

'I want to come too.'

Although the flat in the block on Asparmelur was tiny compared to the house Páll Kampen had built for his family on Mánavallagata, everyone agreed that the storeroom in the basement was a good size. After a bit of a search, the suit turned up in a cardboard box, buried under the collected works of Bjørnstjerne Bjørnson and some old Steamship Company calendars. Hördur was told he could take one of these away with him. He chose the year of his birth and his siblings praised him for his choice. On the front of the calendar was a page of photographs showing the company's activities, printed in blue on thin, yellowish paper, and although they were as grainy as anything printed in that colour on a fuzzy background would be, it was possible to make out a group picture of the stockroom employees in front of the warehouse, with their father Páll second from the right.

Sólveig, Astrid and Gunnar fell silent. Wordlessly, Astrid took the calendar from her little brother's hands and tore out the picture page. Then she handed the calendar back to Hördur, folded the page and stuffed it in the pocket of her skirt.

The suit turned out to be a little on the large side and not exactly in line with the fashions of the day, but with a bit of skill it should be possible to take it in and iron flat the marks where something had previously been sewn onto it. Sólveig, who was in Svavar and Ebba's dance troupe, had grown adept at unpicking seams, taking up, taking in and ironing, since every time new members were admitted to the group, the costumes had to be altered to fit them. Gunnar already had a decent shirt and pair of shoes, and would be permitted to buy himself a tie at the Gentleman's Outfitters.

The plan, put forward by the vicar, was for Erla to hold the reception in the church hall together with two other widows whose children were being confirmed at the same time. But the sisters wouldn't hear of it, saying that there was more than enough to remind their mother of her loss without this to add insult to injury. 'We'll just have to squeeze up,' was all the answer Reverend Ásgeir got when he tried to talk them round.

On the evening of his confirmation day, Gunnar sat on his bed, examining his haul of gifts. He was in his shirt-sleeves, had taken off his tie and undone his top button; the black jacket lay on the bed beside him. There was a set of pens, an envelope containing a hundred and fifty krónur, a copy of Hallgrímur Pétursson's *Hymns of Passion*, an atlas with up-to-date borders, a pen knife, and three volumes of the *Legendary Sagas of the North*. The sound of voices floated up from the floor below where, in the bedroom of the two-room flat, Erla was settling Hördur for the night.

Gunnar had a room to himself in the attic. Although not large, it could accommodate a daybed, a desk and a bookcase, as well as a wardrobe that he referred to as 'the coffin'. There was a skylight that could be opened in the sloping roof and, if he stood on a chair, he could see right over the centre of town to Faxaflói bay. The flat was home to his mother, Hördur and him. Sólveig now lived in the Hlídar area with her boyfriend, a radical history student called Einar, and Astrid rented a place with another girl from her class at the Women's College. It was thanks to this little garret that Gunnar was able to continue living at home with his mother.

33

The party had been a success. With the help of her daughters and a dependable friend, Erla had enjoyed playing hostess for the first time in her new home – which had turned out to be quite large enough, even when the party was at its height. The guests had consisted of Páll's former workmates and their wives and children, Gunnar's friends from their old home in the west end, and their old neighbours. These included Lúther Alfredsson, who had always remained loyal to the Kampen family even after the man of the house had kicked him and called him 'a murderer' the day it was announced on Icelandic radio that the Norwegian resistance writer Nordahl Grieg was dead. Lúther had brought the confirmation boy an illustrated book about insects in German, which, although old, was in good condition.

'E. Jünger, Leipzig 1930'. The dedication on the flyleaf didn't mean anything to Gunnar. Lúther patted him on the back of his hand:

'It's yours now.'

A number of congratulatory telegrams arrived from the Westman Islands, where their closest relatives in Iceland lived. And although they had lost contact with their Norwegian family after the war, the most exciting present had come indirectly from that quarter. It was a package from Buenos Aires, sender: Kirsten Sigrid Kampen, containing a silver-plated cigarette lighter, engraved with the monogram of her favourite nephew.

Gunnar extracted a thick cigar from the breast pocket of his jacket. He opened the skylight and lit the cigar with the lighter. Halli, the stockroom manager, had told him it was a good one, a proper cigar, and, after choking on the first

34

drag, Gunnar soon got the hang of smoking it. On the desk lay a framed Bible quotation, a present from the parish council:

'Lord, I believe. Help thou my unbelief.' — Mark 9:24

Gunnar had, like his fellow confirmation candidates, chosen a text to recite during the ceremony. This was not it. This was one Reverend Ásgeir had imposed on him after forbidding him to utter the words of the Saviour from chapter fourteen, verse twenty-six of the Gospel of St Luke.

II

If any man come to me, and hate not his father,
and mother, and wife, and children, and brethren, and sisters,
yea, and his own life also, he cannot be my disciple.

Luke 14:26

ix

Reykjavík, 26 April 1954

Dear Hjort Helge,

I'll begin by introducing myself. Then you can decide if you want to go on reading this letter or stop here. Of course, I hope you'll do the former but I'll completely understand if it's the latter – in the light of past history. I don't know what restrictions apply to your communication with the outside world but if you do continue reading, I'd be grateful for a reply, even if only a simple confirmation that my letter has reached you. If I don't hear anything, this will at least have given me practice in writing Norwegian, for which I feel a great affection as my second language, although it was never spoken at home. And now you'll probably have guessed who is writing this. I am your nephew, Gunnar Kampen, Páll and Erla's son. (Otherwise I'd never have taken the liberty of addressing you in such a familiar manner.)

Of course, neither the fact that you have a sixteen-year-old nephew in Iceland nor his name will come as news to you,

41

but as my father never talked about you after I grew old enough to understand, I feel I ought to introduce myself as though I were a stranger. Or as I imagine it would be like to introduce oneself to a doppelgänger. From the enclosed photograph you will see that I take much more after you than him. And the resemblance has only become more pronounced since the picture was taken two years ago. For comparison, I have my father's photo of the three of you. It disappeared after Kirsten had been living with us and I assumed, until recently, that it had been thrown away. But my mother brought it out when I started asking about you, and gave it to me. By the way, she speaks well of you, saying that she enjoyed meeting you when she and my father went over to Stavanger so he could show off his Icelandic wife to the family. She said you were cheerful and mischievous. I'm sure she would have asked me to send you her regards if she'd known I was writing to you.

She and I haven't discussed the reasons for the estrangement between yourself and my father. It would be too painful for her. But what makes me all the keener to renew contact with you is the way my father's inner struggle following his decision to disown you eventually broke out in the fatal disease that was to consume him alive. It is something I have thought about a great deal and discussed with close friends. And I'm not alone in seeing the connection. Many other families have lost the man of the house 'in battle' since the war ended. But by my calculations it is more likely to be those who adopted a position on the same side of the battle lines as my father who have fallen prey to the patient internal foe than those who were nourished by the ideals of physical strength and mental alertness. (At least, judging by the way the relationship between views and disease has manifested itself here in Reykjavík.)

But what is he like, this boy Gunnar, who writes to you now, out of the blue?

Let me assure you that I am conscientious and observant, and interested in history, both that of my own country and of the world in general. I look after my health and build up my stamina by cycling and swimming. In May, I will take my school finishing exam and after that I have been offered an apprenticeship as a mechanical engineer. However, I have decided to try my luck at the Commercial College, where I will have the opportunity to improve my knowledge of languages, in addition to learning how to type and handle foreign transactions. I expect this will not be dissimilar to the commercial studies you'll remember from your own schooldays, except that new technology is always being introduced, with the German calculators, in particular, standing out.

Icelanders take a great interest in the affairs of their brother nation. There are a large number of Norwegians living here, as well as people of Norwegian descent like us. Every year, books are published about the recent events, there are talks on the radio and plays are staged. Officially, they all toe the same line. Recently, I was at a meeting of a current affairs club I belong to, where the topic of the day was Norway. After the meeting had finished, a man (Ó.P.), who had known you in Oslo, came over to talk to me. He told me where you were, why you were there and how many years you had left.

Dear Hjort Helge, forgive me for not sending you a parcel. Parcels have to be registered whereas I can stamp and post envelopes myself. I have my own P.O. box (see back), so any correspondence would be strictly between the two of us.

It means a lot to me to be able to extend a reconciliatory hand to you by means of this letter.

Yours sincerely,
Gunnar Kampen

* * *

Reykjavík, 30 June 1954

Dear Hjort Helge,

Little has happened here since I wrote to you in April. I hope you received my letter. Apart, that is, from my sister Sólveig giving birth to a daughter. She was christened after her other grandmother, Merete. I thought you might be pleased to hear that.

Yours sincerely,
your nephew, Gunnar

X

Axel,

Herewith my report.

1) I come from a line of seafaring folk. That's quite clear. My relatives here have lived for so long with the smell of salt in their nostrils, and put away such vast amounts of seafood, that some of them have come to resemble a cross between a man and a fish. Luckily, the women tend to be fish from the waist down and the men from the waist up. (Or should that be the other way round?) And that's not counting the ones who eat nothing but puffin.

But they're kind to me. Goodness, how they pity me for having to live in that den of iniquity, otherwise known as Reykjavík. Are you familiar with the poem, <u>Babylon on Faxi Fjord</u>? I'd never even heard of it before I came here. Now I know it by heart:

In Babylon on Faxi Fjord / the swamp extends on every side, our land lies bound in servitude / the demon drink a rising tide . . .

As they recite this, I nod and think:

'Oh, if only it was half as sinful as you believe!'

Then we wouldn't have to die of boredom all winter, seeking in vain a 'Kaffeehaus' where we could sit in the warm over a steaming cup and talk without the entire place overhearing.

I've been set to work. They go out of their way to see what the sales clerk can endure. Not that I complain, as it's all meant well. When I come back to the mainland, I'll have muscles like Tarzan the Apeman and pockets stuffed with cash. But, crikey, talk about aches and pains!

2) The Turks were here. They burnt down the church and carried off the inhabitants. That was in 1627. As an outsider, you quickly learn not to be flippant about it. I suspect it was this experience that fuelled the town's Christian piety and political activism. What luck that they didn't pick up temperance from the Moors.

3) I mentioned women. I'll say no more. That's your specialist area. But you may add with your yellow pencil, sitting in your red den, that the girls in the Westman Islands are not remotely dazzled by tall, good-natured, neatly groomed, nimble-footed city boys. This is a seasonal fishing station, a dockers' port, and the womenfolk here are far more worldly than most of the nice girls we knew at school.

(Though, having said that, the island maidens are not, it seems, entirely infallible.)

4) There are no Jew— sorry, I mean diamond merchants here.

5) I take back the mockery in my first point. The sea is the land the fisherman must work. He ploughs the waves as the farmer does the soil. One is subject to the caprice of the deep, the other to that of the earth. Sweat falls from both their brows into the element to which they are bound with unbreakable bonds.

Proximity to the merciless sea makes a man stronger. The only pact that can exist between them is the poem by which the individual measures his inner stature against the infinity of the ocean.

6) Now for something that I meant to keep until I saw you, but I just can't hold back. It begins like a ghost story. I sleep off the kitchen, in a pantry that's been converted into a sleeping cupboard. It's the length and height of a man, snugly accommodating one bed with a clothes chest at the foot. (My attic room at home in Melar is palatial by comparison.) There's also a small bookshelf and a lamp over the head of the bed, which means I can stay up and read for as long as I can keep my eyes open.

Anyway, during my first few nights in the cupboard I could have sworn I heard someone moving about in the kitchen in the early hours. I kept starting awake at the sound of creaking floorboards outside the cupboard door. As I was new there, I didn't like to get up and take a look. I didn't want to be caught poking my nose out like some blinking maiden aunt in a school play if it turned out to be nothing more than (my mother's) cousin Árni coming home from a nightshift on the docks.

I propped myself on my elbow and listened, cupping my ear with my hand. Every time I stirred, no matter how quiet I was, the mysterious kitchen visitor moved too, but whenever I stayed still, he or she was silent. This dance of ours was only terminated by my falling asleep in the middle.

Anyway, to cut a long story short, the creaking turned out to be coming from the cupboard itself, or, more precisely, from the mattress I was lying on. Underneath, I found some old newspapers, printed on thin, Depression-era paper, which crackled every time I rolled over. They were issues of the Nazi paper LAND, which came out twenty-four times during the period 1937 to 1938. (As you can guess, I didn't get another wink of sleep until it was time to rise and shine.) One of the men behind the paper, Fridjón, was a friend of the family here, and one of the three sons of Valdimar (Haraldsson), who were all staunch nationalists.

So, I went to visit him. He used to be secretary of the Westman Islands branch of the Party and was responsible for organising the Winter Assistance Fund. Once he was sure that I could be trusted, he showed me keepsakes he had saved from his Party days, including armbands, gramophone records and flags. And I was allowed to take various useful items away with me!

Question: how short should a report like this be? Answer: not too long.

May we meet again, safe and sound, in August, assuming you haven't fallen off your office chair and broken your neck in the meantime, and I haven't been eaten by the locals during their National Festival.

With friendly greetings,
Gunni of the Islands

xi

Reykjavík, 7 October 1956

Dear Editor,

Thank you for the latest issue of <u>The Dawn</u>. As usual it is full of thought-provoking material that will keep me going for a good long while. Whenever I start reading a new issue, it is my practice to have the earlier ones beside me to refer back to when the articles cover similar themes or allude to the same subjects. It wouldn't surprise me to learn that you would appreciate this approach, since I imagine the editor's intention is to build up the reader's knowledge until in the end he feels as if he were standing in a high tower with ideas flocking around him like white birds seeking an exit through the aperture that lets light into the spire. My pile of <u>The Dawn</u> would be that tower.

I do not, however, agree with everything in the journal and wonder if you might consider publishing letters from your subscribers in which we would have a chance to air our views on the issues in question. This ought to be possible without leading to friction since we (only letters by subscribers would be printed) presumably all espouse the same basic standpoint as that expressed in The Dawn:

That the world stands at a watershed. That the reckoning which began ten years ago will be the prelude to the end of civilisation if nothing is done to prevent it. That the omens are obvious to all who have the wit to perceive them, whether they manifest themselves in the hydrogen bomb (used by the apostles of materialism on either side of the Iron Curtain to hold the human spirit hostage); the desire of the coloured man to trade the benefits given to him by Europe (security, training, education and health) for a violent new brand of communism, or the elevation of 'the universally human' at the expense of national values (except among barbarians). That people's attention must be drawn to the ever-increasing hold that 'the Synagogue of Satan' has on the world, through international organisations, Hollywood, major newspapers and universities. That when the dark hour is past, a new day will dawn.

Without losing sight of any of the above, there are two matters to which I would like to draw your attention if you do decide to introduce a column of readers' letters. On the one hand, the journal's vigilance with regard to the alleged cooperation among the Western powers, at least as it appears in your cover picture, and, on the other, the opportunities for resistance to the 'synagogue' that are to be found in our Nordic heritage. I am not sure this would provide sufficient material for two separate letters, since the questions are so inextricably linked in my mind, but I can envisage the letter being in two parts. I believe more-over that it could attract a younger audience to your journal if one of their contemporaries were to write for it, which would be no bad thing.

Perhaps it is a reflection of my youth, but before I discovered your journal I had never found myself simultaneously in agreement and disagreement with the same man. Ever since my political views first crystallised, I have generally been quick to decide whether the person I am talking to is worth engaging with on controversial issues or shared ideas, and then usually discuss only one or the other. So it came as a surprise to me when my barber, Haraldur (Bjarkason – it was at his shop in Adalstræti that I started reading The Dawn), told me that you were a prominent member of the Social Democratic Party. It so happens that my father, Páll Kampen, was active in the party all his life. He was a committed Social Democrat but never sought advancement within the party, saying that all movements had need of ordinary members, because without them they would not be movements so much as fumblings. I don't suppose you'll remember him. I myself used to sell Althýdubladid as a child. I expect our paths first crossed on the pages of that paper, since I learnt to read at an early age and used to devour everything I could lay my hands on.

I hadn't, in other words, expected to find myself in such agreement with a member of my father's party. Or that the Social Democratic movement would have the capacity to recognise the real powers behind those saps who, from ignorance, allow themselves to be used to do the dirty work. I learnt while I was growing up to despise communists and capitalists alike, but I never heard anyone mention then that 'the Synagogue of Satan' was pulling the strings, so successful

53

were they in those days at covering their tracks and blaming their machinations on others. Where we differ, however, is on the question of the extent to which one can perceive the shadow of their grasping claws in our own times.

Dear Editor, I won't keep you much longer. I hope the pains I have taken to write this letter will be apparent to you and that you will judge my reflections as worthy of being printed in The Dawn, should you decide to open up the journal to readers' contributions.

My second reason for writing is to order from you three copies of The Protocols of the Elders of Zion. As you pointed out in your reply to the unbelievably bad article that was printed in the monthly magazine The Northern Lights (which I know only from your report), the book has the tendency to vanish from the shelves of bookshops and libraries. Since it also has a mysterious tendency to fail to return if one lends it out, I have decided that in future I would rather give the book away to my friends than lend it. As before, please send my order to:

G.K., P.O. Box C-93, Reykjavík.

Yours faithfully,
Gunnar Kampen

P.S. It occurs to me that a column of readers' letters could be called 'From the Shore'. For what fairer place exists from which to watch the dawn?

xii

Dear Madame Devi Mukherji,

Thank you for your reply to my letter of September. I am
honoured that you have taken the time to read it and to
respond with such generosity. Deeply honoured. Your parcel
brought with it the fragrance of a far-away world. Far away
and yet so close. A parcel with Indian stamps, postmarked
in Calcutta. I cradled it in my hands as if it were the life-egg
of folk legend (for which the trolls envy mankind, though
they didn't know what to do with it when they had it themselves). On my way home from the post office I paid a visit
to the stamp dealer, Hrafn Karlsson. He is one of the few
people here capable of appreciating the cultural history to
be read from the journey of stamps that have set out from
the ancient homeland of the Aryan race and brought their
cargo safely to its destination in a town founded by a
Norseman who trusted in the heathen gods and his own
strength.

I have read the book ~~three~~ five times from beginning to end and some chapters so often that I have lost count. It more than lives up to its name: <u>Gold in the Furnace</u> is worth its weight in gold. It has been a new experience for me to see things called by their true names. Far too much of what has been written about the rise of Germany and its visionary ideals, about the outstanding individuals who resurrected it from the degradation following the Treaty of Versailles and the populace who gave them their support, about the fall of the Third Reich and the sufferings of the German people after the war, about the need to rewrite the whole story so that it is possible to go forwards – far too much of this has merely been insinuated. (Even in private conversation between people who share the same views, the tendency is to employ irony, euphemisms and evasiveness.) I predict that your book will do much to rectify this.

From the very first page where you dedicate the work to 'the Martyrs of Nuremberg' it was as if you had detonated a depth-charge in my mind. My hands shook. Again and again I had to put the book down. And then came the chapter about your experiences in Iceland.

First, I would like to mention your description of the Hekla eruption, of the power of the merciless lava flow, and how the forces of nature provide us with metaphors to support us in our belief that we are in the service of a law that transcends ordinary man and will, at the moment of truth, summon forth 'the Unique One'. (This chimes with the 'stereoscopic' vision that Ernst Jünger preaches in <u>The Adventurous Heart</u>, which I have tried to adopt in my own life.) And so I vow to you that if Hekla erupts again during our lifetimes I will assemble a force of good men and not only sing praises to the nature spirit but also bring it greetings from Savitri Devi.

My second observation is rather more personal. Your recollection of the party at a house in Reykjavík, where the guests came to the defence of the only Jew present and threw you out of the room, conjured up an old memory. I can't be sure that it was at the same party as the one you describe in <u>Gold in the Furnace</u> (I expect you experienced the same kind of treatment more than once during your stay here) but I am fairly sure that we met during the month you spent in Reykjavík. And I believe I know the identity of the Jew in question.

I was so young when it happened that I had begun to believe I must have dreamt it. But if I'm right, it was at a tea party. In the smart drawing room, the choir director Róbert <u>Abraham</u> Ottósson was holding court, surrounded by sycophants. Finding him loud and disagreeable, without being aware that he was a Jew, I wandered out into the hall (as children do) to explore the rest of the house. You had taken refuge in the library. At least, that's how I remember it.

Ottósson is still here. His influence in the musical world has only increased. After all, he managed to inveigle himself into the state church, like so many of his breed.

In gratitude for your generosity, I have translated into Icelandic the closing speech of Zetut-Neferu-Aton in your play about Akhnaton, which I found in the library of the Theosophy Society. I hope you will appreciate the intention behind my humble effort.

Lands of the North; lands where a bitter wind for ever howls and yells, over ice-bound expanses, under dream-like skies unheard of here; where months of everlasting daylight alternate with months of everlasting night . . . I will sing Thy glory to them all. I will write Thy praise upon the snows of the furthermost shores, and adore Thee in the Midnight Sun. I will make Thee truly King of the South and of the North, for ever.

As I was translating these words I found myself thinking about the many journeys you yourself have undertaken in the last fifteen years, all over the world, to the north and south, preaching your revolutionary view of AkHnaton. (To permit myself an old-fashioned pseudonym.) And to Iceland, of course.

Nothing has changed since you were here, perhaps because so few Icelanders have been personally affected by the injustices of the post-war years. But we do exist. My uncle, Hjort Helge Kampen, is serving a life sentence in a Norwegian prison, and no word has been heard from him despite repeated letters from this end.

Anyway, I look forward to our future exchanges of views. I accept your guidance in the work I am attempting to build up here, together with some friends. They send you greetings from the fray.

Yours in friendship and admiration,
H.H!
Gunnar Kampen

xiii

TELEGRAM

[4 AUGUST 1962 – CHELTENHAM SPA PLC STATION TO
PADDINGTON PLC STATION: ICELANDIC NATIONAL –
DECEASED IN RAILWAY COMPARTMENT – TRAIN ARR.
12.44 PM – ID KNOWN – MOVE TO LONDON MORTUARY
THIS PM – INFORM EMBASSY]

xiv

Dearest Mama,

At last we've got a free day, which gives me a chance to write
to you as I promised. The tour's going well. There's so much
to see here: big cities and smaller towns, museums and parks,
schools and businesses. But in between we've had long days
of travelling. We've covered huge distances compared to what
we're used to in Iceland. Mostly this has been by bus, on
their fantastic autobahns, but also in railway trains, a mode
of travel that is a novelty for us youngsters on our first trip
abroad. A novelty and a pleasure. I can hardly begin to
describe how delightful it is to recline in an elegant, padded
seat by a large viewing window while hurtling through a
forest at two hundred kilometres an hour. With a cup of tea
and an apple strudel. (And all without moving a muscle.)

'It's like being in a film,' said Sveinn from Akureyri.

'Sitting still in one spot, while simultaneously in motion,'
added our tour leader, Hjálmar. In teaching mode, as ever.

The three of us are being well looked after, regardless of whether we came first, second or third in the competition. Wherever we go we're simply introduced as outstanding students of German. Though, to be honest, it took us linguistic geniuses several days to get the hang of speaking the language in normal conversation, and the Germans are tickled by our formality. Which is saying something! As it turned out, I had the least problem with speaking (thanks to all those cycling trips with Lúther), which may explain the equality that exists between the three of us, although the other two have graduated from grammar school (in Akureyri and Reykjavík, respectively), while I 'only' have my diploma from the Commercial College. So I needn't have worried after all.

In the cities, friendship societies have organised introductions to Icelandic culture, at which we read out our prize-winning essays and answer questions from the audience. In the smaller places, we've been given coffee and cakes and repaid the hospitality with songs. Yes, Hjálmar is also in choirmaster mode and I've let myself be persuaded to join in the singing, though I haven't inherited your musical gift.

I don't think it would be doing anyone an injustice to say that the girl in our group has been the star of the trip, and not just because she's blonde and pretty and has a way with words. Her name is Edda (the daughter of Heimir Atlason, the optician) and, as many of the older guests at these events are interested in our medieval literature and the common heritage shared by our two countries, they regard the New Edda as a living answer to the essay question: 'What does the future hold for relations between Iceland and the Federal

Republic of Germany?' (In Cologne, she was actually asked to sign an ancient copy of the <u>Prose Edda</u>!)

Hamburg–Cologne–Frankfurt–Stuttgart–Munich. Everywhere we are welcomed like old friends. I appreciate this kindness all the more in view of the great suffering our hosts endured not so long ago. The destruction of the cities is a silent witness to this, though no one talks about it. The emphasis among these generous people is all on the losses suffered by others.

I am writing to you from a charming little town on the Austrian border. Just over the frontier is Salzburg with all its music. Yesterday we were shown the Dachau concentration camp north of Munich, and today we've been given a free day to spend as we like – a chance to get by in German on our own. I chose to catch a bus heading south, setting off at dawn, with orders, of course, to go to the nearest policeman if I got lost.

From where I'm sitting, there's a view over green forests to the magnificent Alps. They draw the eye from root to summit, to the sky and beyond. It's no wonder that the great men of history have looked to them for inspiration; that here the eagle chooses to build its nest. In comparison, our Esja is no more than a threshold to the city of the gods.

There's only a week left of our tour. On the way home we'll have a two-day stopover in Copenhagen. By the way, my travel fund has come in handy. I have a little something for each of you in my luggage.

Give my love to Sólveig and Astrid.

Your loving son,
Gunnar

P.S. I promised Hördur I'd write to him too. Enclosed is a letter for him. It's about something we discussed before I left.

* * *

Dear Höddi,

I've seen some rabbits but no hares. When I was in the forest, a whole family of rabbits hopped across the path right in front of me. It was a lovely sight.

The other day I thought I saw a hare. Two long, furry grey ears appeared over a garden wall. They moved backwards and forwards, like someone kicking their legs while swimming. That's a giant hare, I thought to myself, and crept up to the wall. Then I heard a pathetic braying. The ears belonged to a donkey! And I was a donkey myself ever to have believed that a hare could be that big.

I've bought you two rabbits. One is white with a brown tail and the other is brown with a white tail. They're both made of chocolate!

Bye, my old mate – onwards and upwards!
Your brother Gunnsi

XV

Reykjavík, 20 April 1958

Party Leader Göran Assar Oredsson,

We, the Icelandic Nationalists, greet you with arms raised high and palms outstretched, and hope that this letter finds you and our other Swedish comrades in the <u>Nordic Realm Party</u> in good heart and full of vigour!

Since you last heard from us we have been organising ourselves, largely in accordance with your recommendations. We are also in contact with Madame Savitri Devi Mukherji (on matters of doctrine) and Commander George Lincoln Rockwell (on dissemination). But the most important news is that we have chosen a name for our party. It is to be called:

<u>THE SOVEREIGN POWER MOVEMENT</u>

Our emblem is the sunwheel. We know that it will please you in the <u>NRP</u> that we have adopted the same symbol as you, except that in our case it will be white on white: fine black lines on a light background. The symbol of the sun as it rekindles after the savage winter, in the instant that it frees the world from its bonds of ice. We are fortunate to have a talented draftsman in our ranks.

It makes such a difference not to have to start all our conversations by explaining that the ideals of the nationalist movement go above and beyond those of the historical phenomenon that disappeared at the end of the war. That they are no more obsolete than any of the other main currents in human history. After all, it wouldn't occur to anyone to write off Christianity on the grounds that it was invented two thousand years ago by a Jew who was murdered by other Jews before his mission could be accomplished. (It's not as if there's any shortage of other reasons!) Now we simply say: 'We are the Sovereign Power Movement. This is our philosophy . . . It is derived in part from . . .' And so on.

Then one thing leads to another and before they know it people have begun to engage with the ideas themselves rather than balking at their origins. The next step in the conversation is to examine the ideas in their historical context. The third is to talk openly about the fact that 'the ideas' are, in fact, the theory of a fundamental law of nature (which itself divides the races) and thus of the evolution of mankind. By then we have come to the core of what we want to safeguard: the right of the Aryan to cultivate his heritage.

Incidentally, the name of the party is the first thing most people want to discuss with us. This is partly because

Icelanders are obsessed with language (they hear at once that this is a new term in Icelandic and they are always excited by innovations), and partly because it brings to mind the concept of the <u>sovereign state</u>. The memory of 1 December 1918, the inauguration of the Icelandic sovereign state, is still alive and well, and our name, the SOVEREIGN POWER Movement, encourages people to ask themselves whether we really have any power, in spite of being a sovereign state. Our answer is: 'No!' A sentiment that many have shared since Iceland became a member of <u>NATO</u> and an American army of occupation was offered a base here – with all the moral and physical corruption this entails – during times of conflict (i.e. for the fore-seeable future. Because when will the world ever be at peace again? Never. Not while the same forces are in control behind the scenes in both the Kremlin and the White House).

With reference to your question:

<u>Socialism</u> is a term we avoid like the plague. It had already become debased in the days of the old Nationalist Party. Here in Iceland, it refers strictly to social democracy or bloodstained bolshevism. Members of the 'old' party who were tricked into using the term national <u>socialist</u> movement now blush and stammer when they are reminded of the fact. We often encounter them at meetings of the Independence Party, where a number of them have holed up and been rewarded with good positions and other such sops. As we explained in our first letter to you, we intend to remain members of the Independence Party until we have managed to recruit sufficient numbers to create a stir when we split off to create our own faction.

Nothing is being done to safeguard our Icelandic cultural heritage. The Nordic Association in Reykjavík is utterly toothless. The Icelandic department at the university has until recently been run by a drug addict. They have appointed a poet of obscene verses as director of the National Museum. Our last Director of Radio was a spiritualist.

Nor is there any help to be had from the only Icelander who unquestionably met the Führer. The author, Gunnar Gunnarsson, developed amnesia when he 'fled' Denmark a week before the German invasion. These days he is America's poodle, letting himself be used in the fight against global communism. (That's his penance, and I suppose it could be worse.)

Thank you for your examples of how you respond to exaggerations about the concentration camps: we will bear them in mind. The Jews in Iceland keep their heads down and have hitherto avoided attracting attention by publicising their sufferings. But we can assume that this weapon will be used against us once we grow in strength.

The most indomitable warriors of the Varangian Guard in Constantinople (Mikligardur) were those from Sweden and Iceland. Our nations are destined to unite against the criminal hordes, to raise aloft our flapping sunwheel standards (black/red/white) and march to war.

Long live free Greater Europe!

With fraternal greetings,
Gunnar Kampen, Leader
Axel St. Gudmundsson, Deputy Leader

Hólmar Jónasson, Treasurer
Sigurhanna Hallgrímsdóttir, Secretary

(THE SOVEREIGN POWER MOVEMENT,
P.O. BOX C-93,
REYKJAVÍK,
ICELAND)

xvi

Reykjavík, 22 September 1959

My dear Hanna,

How is Royal Copenhagen? No, don't tell me. I'd only be jealous if I heard about your life in the <u>Babylon on Øresund</u> and your days at the <u>Rigshospitalet</u>. The lurid covers of the Danish doctor–nurse romances in Sigfús Eymundsson's bookshop tell me all I need to know about the pleasures in store for a pretty nursing auxiliary. Whereas in the Icelandic bank romances, which they must surely stock in <u>Boghallen</u> on Rådhuspladsen, you'll be able to read about the heart-break of a young bank clerk. It has in no way diminished since you were last here over a month ago.

Yes, you're sorely missed here in Ingólfur Arnarson's settlement. Who by? Me, of course. (Ingólfur died over a thousand years ago.) If we were in a romantic poem I would say that the plants of the earth and the birds of the air, the fish in the sea and the beasts in the forest miss you too; the Reykjavík version being the dandelion, the blackbird, the haddock and the cat. But our romantic poem is over. Don't you think I'm taking it well? Given how much I miss you?

Et Digt er som en Kilde, der risler frem først længe efter at Regnen er faldet. (A poem is like a spring, which only trickles forth long after the rain has fallen.) – Jóhann Sigurjónsson

Of course, I would never have been able to go abroad with you. (Even if you'd wanted me to.) We have favourable winds for our cause and the time is nigh when we'll be able to step forth as a fully fledged modern nationalist party. It's happening all over the world, in Europe and America. We're constantly receiving messages of encouragement from well-wishers near and far. But since Axel's betrayal, the work here in Iceland has largely fallen on my shoulders. My aspirations are for the cause above all else and I believed that his heart beat for it too. But the promise of thirteenth place on the list of candidates in the forthcoming City Council elections turned out to be all it took to weaken his faith. (Wasn't Judas the thirteenth man at the table?) The rest of us are set to resign from the Independence Party on 20 December. (The anniversary of the day on which the last issue of Iceland, the journal of the old Nationalist Party, came out in the winter of 1938.) At the same time we will formally become a chapter of the NRP.

I have the flat on Asparmelur to myself these days. Mother has moved out to Selfoss to be closer to Hördur now that he has a place at the Sólheimar Home for the Mentally Disabled. He will be well cared for there among the other 'adult children' and this will hopefully give her more time to herself. She's got a job on the cheese production line at the Flóamenn Dairy, which is said to be the most technologically advanced in the country. On clear days she can see her beloved Westman Islands rising from the sea on the horizon.

I intend to keep the flags and other sensitive material in my old attic room, together with my memories of you – of the time we spent there. It will be my shrine. The headquarters will be in the sitting room downstairs. Karl acquired a second-hand table and chairs from 'a friend' in the law department. Books and magazines will be displayed on the table, and there will be hot coffee in the thermos every evening from 7 p.m. onwards. We won't be homeless any more and will be able to talk as loudly as we like.

Hanna, when you left, I lost not only a girlfriend but a comrade in ideals. (In you, we also lost the only girl in our party. What is it with Icelandic women and politics? Where are they?) Who is there now to share with me the letters of support from Rockwell, written as he tears from state to state in his station wagon, uniting white men against the onslaught of blacks and Jews – with Thóra and the children in the trailer? Do you remember him telling us how they spent a whole day in the lunatic asylum with Ezra Pound? And how you went to the library to borrow a copy of his poems because we thought they would be full of fascist sentiments. Such a load of nonsense. (Their marriage is over, by the way. Her family forced them apart with the help of the Masonic clique. George Lincoln came to Iceland recently to win her back. It was heroic. It was tragic.)

Now I know you'll be saying to yourself: 'He hasn't mentioned a word about his illness.' You're right. I decided not to. All you need to know is that for the moment I'm fine. What gives me strength on all fronts is missing you and remembering what we had together.

Your 'ex' but eternal friend,
Gunni

P.S. A little gossip to finish up with. Our old schoolmate, Alfred Nielsen, has been causing a furore here. No one's ever heard anything like the stuff he's been coming out with about his colleagues and about art in general. Abstract art has come in for a particularly severe bashing, whereas he himself is apparently a seer and a genius. Of course, this was merely a ploy to advertise his show in the Bogasalur Gallery at the National Museum. It worked. The show's selling out!

I find A.N.'s pictures repellent. They are rotten and present man as an abject creature. Everyone is depicted as grotesque and subject to the basest of urges. Yet at the same time they're so fresh and bold. He doesn't hesitate to turn the clock back even as he rings in the future. Although the artists he names as his influences are men that no self-respecting society would have allowed to walk free, I feel that he is laying down the same kind of challenge to his contemporaries as I want to achieve with the Party. But in a diametrically opposed manner!

In his extraordinary interview in <u>The People's Will</u> (don't worry, I didn't buy a copy, I read it at Café Hressó), it emerges that he's currently in the same part of the world as you, studying at the Royal Academy in Copenhagen. I'm only telling you this so that you can cross to the opposite fortov, should you run into our Alfred.

Yours, G.

P.P.S. Although I long ago lost patience with the editor of The Dawn's obsession with Christian numerology, perhaps he's onto something when he claims that we're re-living the conflicts of the thirties and forties? (See: Degenerate Art.) The outcome of the Third World War will be in our youthful hands.

The people's stamina is so exhausted that they have begun to fear the worst. Thus it is our duty to carry out a post-mortem on the causes and arm ourselves against the powers of darkness which are at work here.

Sigurjón Sigurdsson, *Mjölnir*, 1st issue, 1936

xvii

The list was delivered to P.O. Box C-93. The envelope was brown, addressed to 'The SP Movement c/o G. Kampen', but there was no sender. The stamp had been postmarked at the Langholt branch of the post office – '-11.V.1960' – which conveyed nothing to Gunnar. Anyone could have gone there to post the letter, whether or not they lived in Reykjavík.

The heading was 'ENEMIES OF ICELAND – 1ST CATEGORY, JEWS'. Listed in alphabetical order, on two typewritten pages, were the names of Jews domiciled in the Greater Reykjavík area, in Akureyri and in other towns around the country, together with their addresses, occupations and ages. Corrections and additions had been made in three different hands: crossings out, exclamation and question marks, abbreviations, changes to letters that didn't exist on Icelandic typewriters – for example 'o' had been corrected to the Danish 'ø' in Møller – and several names had been marked with stars of David, from one to five, according to some unexplained system. From the telephone numbers it was apparent that the list had been compiled before 1949, since Reykjavík numbers had been lengthened

by the addition of another digit since then. The typeface
was pale violet, with a faint capital K; clearly a carbon copy.
Altogether the list consisted of thirty-four names, some of
which were already familiar to Gunnar:

Abrahams
Edelstein
Kroner
Löwe
Mann
Rosenthal
Sonnenfeld
Urbancic
Wang
Zier

Seeing so many of them together like this filled him with a
sudden fury, similar to the feeling he had experienced when
told that what he had taken to be no more than normal
aching bones and fatigue were in fact the first symptoms of
myeloma. Many of those on the list would have had children
since it was made – with Icelanders too.

Ever since the founding of the Sovereign Power Movement,
there had been a consensus among the members of the
executive committee that they would not prioritise the fight
against domestic Jews. They had enough on their plate in
combating 'the intellectual Jews' who threatened the freedom
of ordinary Icelanders from the right and left, Marxists and
capitalists, as well as those, such as avant-gardists and jazz
musicians, who committed atrocities against the nation's
cultural heritage.

The Jewish question was complicated in Iceland. Gunnar had discussed it with laymen and experts, both indirectly and openly. As far as he could discover, pure-bred Jews had played almost no part in the history of Iceland over the centuries. However, many of those with whom he had discussed the subject suspected that a number of the 'Danish' merchants who for two hundred years had sucked the life-blood out of the impoverished smaller nation, fobbing them off with rotten foodstuffs, crawling with maggots, had in fact been Jews who had acquired their licence to trade as a result of their conversion to Christianity. This was hard to prove without combing the archives of the Royal Library in Copenhagen, and as yet no one had undertaken this research, but it could hardly be a coincidence that the adjective 'Jewish' also signified 'miserly'. The Icelanders' only other acquaintance with the true nature of the race was through the beloved *Hymns of Passion*, which gave a clear account of their deceitfulness and malice.

The present situation was very different. Following the introduction of religious freedom by King Christian IX's constitution of 1874 – contrary to the wishes of the Icelanders – the eternally wandering race had started fetching up in dribs and drabs in the last place on earth that could be considered their natural home. Jew after Jew had straggled over the sea from the slums of Copenhagen, to which the vermin had once again begun making their way across the European landmass from various god-forsaken holes in the Orient.

Then there had been that big jump in the thirties, when the Third Reich began to purge itself of Jews. Gunnar had read up on the subject in contemporary newspaper accounts.

The Icelandic nationalists had fallen asleep on their watch, placing their trust in the Minister of Justice, Hermann Jónasson, leader of the Progressive Party and a well-known enthusiast for the purity of his nation. Yet, although the minister had done all in his power to halt the tide, evidently a sizeable group had made it to the white island, sinking their claws into Icelandic soil. The list of names bore witness to that.

After reflecting on the matter for several days, Gunnar came to the conclusion that, although the list was out of date, the information it contained was nevertheless too incendiary to be shared with ordinary members of the Sovereign Power Movement, some of whom were a little 'hot-headed'.

He therefore summoned a meeting, inviting, in addition to his two fellow committee members – deputy leader Hólmar Jónasson and secretary Matthías Lange – the party's security officer, Pétur Bergmann. All agreed that the list bore the signs of having been a confidential document and that it should remain so. It was decided that the four of them would form a committee charged with updating the list. A special file would be created for all Jews in Iceland over the age of sixteen. Gunnar, whose job at the bank gave him access to the National Register, would plough through it during his coffee breaks to obtain the Jews' current addresses. Hólmar, who was an amateur photographer, undertook the task of photographing everyone on the new list with the help of his zoom lens. Pétur would drive him around since he had a black Volkswagen Beetle and was free at weekends. Matthías, meanwhile, would help Gunnar to add the new information. The document would be kept in the attic room at Asparmelur, in the same locked cupboard as the list of party members.

Göran Assar Oredsson had set the Sovereign Power Movement the condition of taking purposeful action on the Jewish issue before they could be recognised as a full chapter of the Nordic Realm Party. This obstacle had now been removed.

They decided on the name 'Operation 5 October', abbreviated to 'O.V.O.', for the mission, in commemoration of the day, a year previously, when Hjort Helge Kampen had been found hanged in his cell at Oslo's Botsfengselet Prison.

xviii

They stand by the window overlooking the lake, their backs
to the bright summer's day outside. Light falls on their
cheeks, necks and shoulders, but their faces and bodies are
indistinct in the muted tones of the half-shadow. How long
is it since the three of them were last alone together, the
elder Kampen siblings, Sólveig, Astrid and Gunnar? Shouldn't
it be more fun than this?

'Has Lúther been round yet?'

'I didn't know I was expecting him.'

The silhouette exaggerates the sisters' familiar movements
and the outlines of their arms, which appear to be growing
out of their middles. Both swivel their right hands as they
talk, tilting them back at the wrist and pointing into the air
with bent index fingers, which they then wave in a circle for
emphasis. Whenever one is speaking, the other swivels her
hand in sympathy – but never in time – as if recalling a
dance they mistakenly believe they once danced together.

'He's in town.'

'At the loony bin?'

'That's not funny.'

'At a synod.'

Astrid leans against the window sill. A cloud passes before the sun, extinguishing the red lights in her pinned-up hair. Sólveig steps forward and starts rearranging the flowers in the vase on the table beside the sickbed. They have brought him a white bouquet, made up of carnations supported by unnaturally green grasses – too long, thin and dry to produce a note if blown. As if there were any need for more whiteness in these institutional surroundings where everything is white, unless it is green.

'Mum asked him to look in on you.'

'Then he'll come.'

'She thinks it would do you good to listen to him.'

'Or the opposite.'

The sisters both now move away from the window and sit down on either side of Gunnar's bed. He turns his head from one to the other.

'What do carnations smell like?'

'What did he say?'

'The carnations, what do they smell like?'

Sólveig pulls a carnation from the vase, shakes the water off the stem and holds it out to Gunnar. He lies back against his pillow without taking it.

'You'll have to tell me. I can't smell anything.'

'Like a carnation.'

'But I can't remember. Honestly.'

Sólveig raises the flower to her nose and sniffs. Then she reaches across the bed so Astrid can inhale the scent too. Astrid closes her eyes and thinks. Then she pats the bed.

'Like you.'

'Me?'

'Back when you were a good little boy and had just got out of the bath.'

Raindrops rattle against the window. Outside, the sky has turned an ominous grey.

'Why didn't Einar come in?'

'He took the kids to the park.'

'What's happening there?'

'It's the seventeenth of June!'

'In here it's just an ordinary Friday.'

'Not from what I can hear.'

The sound of a radio is coming from behind the green curtain that has been drawn between Gunnar's bed and that of his neighbour, who is listening to the National Day programme. Two men are discoursing in sombre tones about the last days of the Enlightenment figure, Eggert Ólafsson: 'An original poet; one shouldn't forget the fantastical *Sukkudokkaland*.' Their sentences are punctuated by choking noises. It's impossible to tell if the neighbour is coughing or laughing.

The siblings fall silent, fighting back the urge to giggle.

After Sólveig and Astrid had left, Gunnar asked to see the ward doctor and told him that if an elderly man came to see him – grey-haired, stooping, with a . . . what do you call it again? . . . a beard round his mouth; his name's Reverend Lúther Alfredsson – he was to be informed that Gunnar was too ill to receive visitors; that he was weak from the drugs he was taking, that he was asleep, or some similar excuse. They would know how to put it without telling the man bluntly that he was unwelcome here.

The doctor understood. He would let the nurses know.

This was a sanatorium. The most important thing was for the patients to be left in peace.

As time had passed following Germany's defeat, Lúther's faith in the Third Reich had gradually weakened. For the first ten years he had given no hint of what was happening, but on New Year's Day in 1956, he had suffered a nervous breakdown. When he came home from the mental hospital, he had enrolled in the theology department at the university and went on to become their oldest ever graduate. He was given a small living in the parish next door to his birthplace in the south of Iceland, which made him a neighbour once more of Erla Kampen, just like in the old days.

Reverend Lúther blamed himself for Gunnar's infatuation with nationalism and lost no opportunity to try to make him see sense. As news of the Adolf Eichmann trial started coming in, he had grown increasingly frantic.

Gunnar had had enough of his sermons.

xix

NEW MJÖLNIR

The *New Mjölnir*, named after Thór's hammer, is the newsletter of the Sovereign Power Movement and the NRP in Iceland.

Publisher: Gunnar Kampen.
Price for non-subscribers: 5 krónur.

A QUESTION FOR EUROPE ALONE TO ANSWER

The power and strength to save Europe reside in Europe alone. The question of German reunification is one that neither Kennedy nor Khrushchev have an exclusive right to answer. The other European nations must recognise Germany as the heart of Europe. It is our bulwark against the barbarian in the East and our only defence against the corrupt trade policies of the West that do nothing but inflict poverty and misery on Europe.

Treacherous European politicians have turned the

Continent into a chessboard on which brother nations are played off against one another in a dangerous game. We must sweep these mediocre politicians out of the way and replace them with men capable of thinking and working in the spirit of European nationalism.

FROM ARTICLE 2 OF OUR MANIFESTO
An Icelandic citizen is someone who is born of Icelandic parents. The right to Icelandic citizenship should only be granted to those who are of Nordic or closely related stock, who become assimilated into the culture of our nation.

NATIONALISTS
The Sovereign Power Movement's winter programme will commence in September with a meeting and a social evening. Events to include: the appointment of the new committee of NORDIC YOUTH, with a report to be delivered by the outgoing chairman. Speeches, a film show, messages from supporters, battle songs, readings, generous refreshments, and more. Details of the location and date of the meeting will be sent out to members shortly.

THE LIGHTNING AND THE SUN
We have Savitri Devi's book on Adolf Hitler for sale. Price per copy: 20 krónur.

YOUNG PEOPLE OF ICELAND! THE SOVEREIGN POWER MOVEMENT IS A YOUTH MOVEMENT!
Fight with the Sovereign Power Movement for a free, united and independent EUROPE. Fight with us against international communism and global Zionism, which threaten our

white civilisation. Protest against nuclear testing by East and West. Protest against the use of Europe as a battleground by Russia and America. Protest against Iceland's membership of NATO. Be warned that if a Third World War breaks out, Europe will bear the brunt. That is why nationalists must band together under the emblem of the sunwheel.

Enrolment in the movement is handled by its leader, Secretary General of the Nordic Realm Party in Iceland. Applications should be sent to P.O. Box C-93, Reykjavík.

THE FUTURE

The Sovereign Power Movement cannot at present operate as an official political party. All our activities have to be carried out behind closed doors. But it is our hope that we will soon be able to bring our work into the open and grow into a powerful popular front. If we find that people recognise the value of our cause, we will not hesitate to increase our visibility accordingly.

It is vital that members are active in disseminating the fair ideals which underpin our movement.

NORTHERN EUROPEAN RING

The Sovereign Power Movement works closely with fraternal parties abroad. The Northern European Ring is a transnational organisation of Westerners who are dedicated to preserving the Germanic race and the Aryan heritage. The NER is made up of a large number of organisations and individuals from all over the world, including Germany. The organisation's newsletter, The Northern European, is available from selected bookshops in Reykjavík as well as from the NER agent in Iceland. (See P.O. box elsewhere in this newsletter.)

FOREIGN NEWS

1) The MSI (neo-fascists) increased their following by 28% in the Italian municipal elections. Needless to say, there wasn't a single word about this major victory in Iceland's Jewish-run press.

2) Zorlu, the former Turkish foreign secretary, who was recently executed for multiple crimes, was for more than a decade one of the most influential figures in the North Atlantic Treaty Organisation.

3) The American Nazi Party has greatly expanded its activities and membership base, which now stands at some 1,500 people. The contribution of the party leader, Commander Lincoln Rockwell, has been invaluable to the cause. He was previously an officer in the American army at Keflavík air base and is familiar with local conditions in Iceland. Last summer Rockwell was planning a visit to the Sovereign Power Movement but the Zionist authorities here denied him a travel visa. This is virtually unheard of and entirely a consequence of the growing support for the Nationalists.

4) Wiking-Jugend held a well-attended rally on 19–20 May at Hirsau in the Black Forest. Pictures to follow in the next issue.

5) Mildred Gillars, who worked for German radio during the war under the name of 'Axis Sally', was recently released from prison in West Virginia. She had served a 12-year sentence and is now 60 years old.

6) The NS Boerenasie in South Africa have joined the NER.

7) Paraguay is now home to many freedom fighters from Europe, who have escaped the clutches of the bloody-handed executioners and kidnappers of the Israeli State.

A POPULAR FRONT IS THE ONLY WAY!

XX

'And have you been happy here at the bank?'

Wood-panelled walls of stone. Paintings by Jóhannes Kjarval and Ásgrímur Jónsson. Forests of lava. The carpet thick and green, like moss that was slowly but surely devouring the furnishings. In two corners of the office there were tall plants in wide-bellied terracotta pots decorated with oriental motifs. Between them a ceiling-high bookcase, divided into many sections, held statute books, annual reports and anthologies of prose and poetry in Icelandic and other languages, while in the middle there was a shelf closed off behind glass, on which could be seen a palm-sized oblong frame containing a photograph so old and faded that one could only just make out the portrait of a man with protruding eyes and a chin beard, on which the subject himself had written in an adroit hand, in ink that had lasted rather better than he had: 'Dear Konrád, look how ugly I've become. Your friend, Jónas.'

At the far end of the room stood the managing director's desk, on a carved base of dark, varnished mahogany; seen from the door, it resembled the façade of an antique temple in the Nile Valley. The desk top, which was over three metres long and ninety centimetres wide, was covered with the red, cured leather of a whale penis, held in place by straight rows of dome-headed studs, which marched round the edge like slaves shouldering sacks of gold. There was a reading lamp with a shade of Venetian glass; a pile of unopened letters on a silver salver; a set of pens on a marble stand with an inlaid map of the world, the three pen holders placed in New York, Moscow and Jerusalem; a stack of stock exchange news in various languages; and a Bible. Behind the desk was an upholstered chair with a back that curved around the person sitting in it and thickly padded arms, ideal for supporting one's fore-arms and hands while one was making carefully considered decisions or issuing orders with perfect sangfroid. On the hand-woven rug in front of the desk, two visitors' chairs were placed at slight angles to ensure that the occupants would be comfortably in the sightline of the person who had summoned them to the meeting.

'In the circumstances, I mean.'

When Gunnar Kampen, clerk in the foreign exchange department, was shown into the office of Bjarni Ólafsson, managing director of the National Bank, the director, instead of motioning him to one of the visitors' chairs, had risen from his own imposing seat, come round from behind the desk and invited Gunnar to take a deep leather chair by the window overlooking Austurstræti, while he planted himself on the chesterfield sofa facing him. The director's secretary brought them a tray of afternoon refreshments,

Earl Grey and *kleinur*, which she placed on the coffee table between them.

'I take mine without milk.'

The managing director blew on the sliver of lemon floating on the steaming surface of his tea before taking a sip. Then he pointed to the doughnut twists:

'These are very good *kleinur*.'

Gunnar nodded:

'Yes, I've been happy here.'

In spite of the loss of appetite caused by the latest round of drugs, he took a doughnut and made a show of nibbling it. The managing director continued:

'Then I hope you'll understand that we only want the best for you.'

For more than six months Gunnar had been waiting for a summons from on high, ever since he had led seventeen members of the Sovereign Power Movement in the ceremonial laying of a wreath on the memorial to German fighter pilots shot down off the Icelandic coast during the war. The ceremony had taken place on the first day of summer, which this year had fallen on 20 April, Adolf Hitler's birthday. They had assembled in the cemetery under the swastika ensign of the Third Reich navy, chosen from Gunnar's collection for its similarity to the Nordic national flags – especially that of Norway – and to emphasise that this was the first time for twenty-three years that Icelanders had openly recognised the holy symbol of the Aryans. *Althýdubladid*, mouthpiece of the Social Democrats, had printed an article about 'Nazi youth' on the march, while *Vísir* had published a photograph of the members in the act of giving the Hitler salute. The tone of the entire coverage had been mocking. The *Althýdubladid* reporter, in particular, had gone out of his way to ridicule Gunnar by quoting offensive passages from his speech. In the following months, Gunnar had leaked various bits of information about their activities to the reporter, who had immediately worked them up into articles. Which only went to show that the fool had no idea he was being used. Every time the words 'Heil Hitler!' were attributed to Gunnar Kampen on the pages of the newspaper, the Sovereign Power Movement gained a new member. The latest leak had been typewritten on headed stationery from the National Bank of Iceland, with a white sunwheel stuck over the bank's logo. On reflection, that had been a mistake.

The managing director, Bjarni Ólafsson, drew himself up:

'The bank would like to invite you to take paid leave until you have recovered your health. Should you choose to seek treatment abroad, the union's sickness benefit fund will provide financial support for your trip.'

Gunnar turned over the lump of doughnut with his dry tongue. By taking a mouthful of over-sweet tea, he managed to wet the piece enough to swallow it. He could feel it burning its way down to his stomach. Carefully, he got up from the leather chair and, once his dizzy spell had passed, said:

'I'm grateful to the bank.'

The managing director rose to his feet, came over to Gunnar and clasped his hand.

'I'm glad to hear it.'

Gunnar's gaze fell on the window. A famous photograph of the old Nazi party had been taken from this angle on 1 May 1936, when a hundred men in brown shirts had marched through the centre of town. He happened to know that the managing director, now escorting him to the door, had been one of the flag-bearers that day.

xxi

NEO-NAZI ON STOPOVER

13.2.1962. *Althýdubladid* learnt yesterday that a member of the international neo-Nazi movement paid a visit to Iceland at the weekend. The individual in question is one Poul Engelen. He flew here from Luxembourg on an Iceland Airways plane, landing at Keflavík Airport on Saturday, before continuing his onward journey yesterday.

He is alleged to have been on his way to a meeting with George Lincoln Rockwell, who has achieved notoriety in the United States for his Nazi Party, and indeed Engelen asked staff at the airport whether any of them were familiar with Rockwell's name. He also attempted to get people to talk about politics but received little encouragement. Eventually, he asked where he could find Gunnar Kampen, the ringleader of a small group of neo-Nazis here in Iceland. He was given assistance in making contact with the Icelandic Führer, after which Engelen travelled to Reykjavík where he spent much of Sunday.

Yesterday, as mentioned above, Engelen continued his journey to New York to meet Rockwell. This is thought to be the first time since the war that Nazis have travelled openly between countries with a stopover in Iceland.

Tuesday. Hólmar dropped by Asparmelur with a copy of the paper. The doorbell rang in one long and three short bursts. He didn't have time to stop for a coffee as his father was waiting for him outside the building in the Goldfish Bowl delivery van. They were on their way down to the harbour to collect a consignment of zebrafish or zebra finches – Gunnar didn't quite catch which – from the Steamship Company warehouse.

The article was more restrained than usual. The only snide comments made by the Sovereign Power Movement's useful dupe of a reporter were when he referred to Gunnar as the 'Führer' and described the party as 'a small group'. Gunnar didn't let it get to him. What mattered was the information provided at the beginning and end of the piece:

That there was 'an international neo-Nazi movement'. That its representatives were 'travelling openly between countries' and that Iceland was one of their stopping-off points.

And that they had a representative here in Gunnar Kampen.

People would notice.

At lunchtime on Sunday, Poul Engelen had come to town in an Adalstöd taxi and taken a room at Hótel City. On meeting in the hotel reception, he and Gunnar had been pleasantly surprised to discover that they were around the same age. The foreigner had sounded more mature when they spoke on the phone the previous evening, thanks to his warm, baritone voice. And it had probably been the slow, slightly hesitant delivery – the result of his latest treatment – that had made Gunnar sound older than usual.

Their acquaintance was put on an even more intimate footing by the visitor's suggestion that they use first names: it would be in keeping with the fraternal spirit of the nationalist movement. They could be Engelen and Kampen, even Herr Engelen and Herr Kampen, in other people's hearing.

On the pavement outside the hotel, Gunnar asked the visitor:

'What would you like to do?'

Poul said he'd like to talk.

And so the day passed in conversation between two ardent souls, meeting for the first time, who burned with zeal for the same cause. They began by ordering open sandwiches and beer at Braudbær, then moved on to the café at 11 Laugavegur – where a shaky-handed bohemian shouted: 'If it isn't Mini-Hitler!', only to subside sheepishly on his bench when he realised that Gunnar was in the company of a foreigner – and from there they had strolled through Thingholt and the streets named for the heathen gods; Lokastígur, Týsgata, Thórsgata, Ódinsgata and Urdarstígur – Poul was speechless with delight over these names – down Bragagata to Lake Tjörnin, through the park, past the National Museum and the main building of the university, which they agreed would make a fine *Reichstag*, and from there it had been but a short walk to the headquarters in Melar.

It was the first opportunity Gunnar had ever had for a serious discussion of his philosophical ideas. And in German too. The tiredness lifted from his shoulders and he felt lighter in spirit than he had for years.

At home on Asparmelur, Gunnar cooked them haddock and potatoes with melted butter. Poul was pleased with this plain Icelandic meal, saying he would gladly break his rule of eating only vegetarian fare for the privilege of tasting proper Viking food. While they were eating, he described the battle he and the Flemish Nazi youth were waging for the humane treatment of farm animals and the protection of wildlife and the natural habitat. His party included many committed believers in naturalism.

Shortly after eight, they were joined by Hólmar and Pétur, the security officer. Gunnar immediately regretted inviting them over. Neither spoke German and most of their English had been picked up from American films. Every topic of discussion seemed diminished by their presence, whether they contributed to the conversation or merely sat there dumbly staring at the visitor.

The high point of the evening came when Gunnar showed Poul a newspaper cutting with a photo of a fair-haired man standing at the side of Vidkun Quisling.

Poul was moved to say:

'If I didn't know better I'd think it was you.'

Gunnar told him the story of his uncle, Hjort Helge Kampen, and Poul nodded. Similar events had happened in his own family. But it was the first time Gunnar's Icelandic comrades had heard the reason for Hjort Helge's life sentence: when members of the Norwegian resistance had turned up to arrest him for collaborating with the Gestapo, he and Emma, his German wife, had decided to take the strychnine pills he kept concealed in the swastika ring on the middle finger of his right hand. She had been successful;

he had not. Hjort Helge had received two sentences: seven years for 'treason' and life for Emma's murder.

At midnight, Herr Kampen had accompanied Herr Engelen back to Hôtel City. There they had said their good-byes and promised to meet again the following autumn in England, at the formal inauguration of the World Union of National Socialists. The purpose of Poul's present travels was to have private discussions with various parties about the planned international summit.

After this, Gunnar had gone home and slept until the doorbell rang with one long and three short bursts on Tuesday, thirty-six hours later.

xxii

A whorl of blond hair curling to the right in the middle of his neck and another, smaller one higher up on the left of his crown. Contrary to all conventional wisdom, it had started growing back after he began his treatment in the radiology department in London. In four weeks it had sprouted enough for one student nurse to offer him a haircut. They both knew she only said this to cheer him up but it was a game he was quite happy to play along with.

Gunnar had noticed that she went out of her way to be kind to him – the young, dying man, who had no visitors apart from one elderly gentleman who came every five days to sit with him in the visitor's lounge. His name was Richard and, although he was from Wales, he belonged to the local Icelandic Society. The members organised visits to any of their compatriots who came to London in search of medical treatment. Thirty years ago, Richard had had an Icelandic friend who had gone home for a short visit one summer and never returned, or, as he put it in his extraordinarily good Icelandic: 'That's what you Icelanders are like. Once you go home, you disappear into thin air.'

Gunnar appreciated the student nurse's efforts.

'Sit still!'

She draped a sheet around him and plied the 'dog clippers' with professional skill.

In reality, she took no more than five millimetres off the sides and two off the top but that was enough to be able to call it a short back and sides. Gunnar had started shaving again and for the last two weeks he had found it easier to recognise the man in the mirror.

One morning he asked:

'Am I some sort of miracle?'

'Ask Richard.'

Said Jackie, whose proper name was Jacqueline, although she wasn't French, as Gunnar had supposed, but a native of St Lucia. She had worked at a hairdresser's salon on the island and used to cut her father's and brothers' hair at home.

'We're all miracles.'

Was Richard's reply when he appeared in the visitor's lounge several days later. It was the last time he was to sit there with Gunnar, carrying on a conversation with himself about the Icelanders' propensity to vanish. At the end of the visit he took his leave with a quotation from Dylan Thomas's *Under Milk Wood*:

Oh, angels be careful there with your knives and forks.

It would not be long now before Gunnar vanished too and his soul became the fodder of heavenly beings, if one believed in such things. He had no illusions about what awaited him here on earth. Although the doctors treated him like a rare specimen – in their white coats, standing behind leaded glass to protect them from the gamma rays – his fate was inevitable. Even the sophisticated cobalt-60 teletherapy machines in Her Majesty's oncology ward did not have the power to destroy the enemy lurking in his bones. The painkillers he was administered grew stronger, the moments when his mind was clear ever fewer and further between. Apart from the unexpected re-growth of his hair, there had been no detectable signs of success.

His grey eyes developed a feverish glaze, his pupils were dilated and sometimes he wore sunglasses indoors. In the evenings, he watched television with the other patients. News, nature programmes, science programmes, documentaries, quizzes, slapstick comedies and football; all seemed as novel to him as there being no television in Iceland was to the others – and went some way towards compensating him for not having had a chance to see anything of the city beyond the vicinity of the hospital, where those who felt up to it were taken for a breath of fresh air in the park a stone's throw away.

There was a lot going on in London. Since Gunnar had arrived at the end of June, there had been two large public rallies, each held by a different nationalist movement; one in the Jewish area in the East End, the other in Trafalgar Square, no less. From the news reports it was easy to guess who was in charge at the BBC, since the focus was all on the opposition to those attending the rallies, and on justifying the violence to which they had been subjected by Bolsheviks and Jews.

They had the same colour eyes, Gunnar and Jackie. It hadn't crossed his mind that she was a mulatto until she told him where she came from. A sign of his lack of sophistication.

But Gunnar Kampen hadn't come to England to look his own mortality – or a student nurse from the Caribbean – in the eye.

Seven days before he discharged himself from hospital, he began forcing down whole meals. He built up his strength still further by making all his perambulations around the hospital unaided. He also reduced his intake of the drugs that made him confused.

With the help of the *A–Z* street map of Greater London, he measured his strength against the distances he would need to cover on foot and calculated that it would be sufficient.

There was a public telephone booth in the visitor's lounge, from which one could make national calls using coins, although international ones had to be booked 'collect'. The first phone call Gunnar made on Friday 3 August was brief:

'Yes, it's me. I expect to be with you early, about half-past seven. Thank you for that. Thank you.'

The second was longer and ended with Gunnar telling his mother not to worry, that everything would be all right. Hördur was visiting her for the weekend, so he got to talk to him too.

'Bye, my old mate – onwards and upwards!'

xxiii

The Icelandic Embassy was located within walking distance of the hospital. He had allowed himself twenty minutes to get there but decided to take it slowly and savour his moment in the city. The streets were empty, apart from the night buses that roared past at regular intervals.

The sky was turning blue with the dawn when Gunnar rounded the corner of Eaton Terrace. On the building's white façade he saw the arms of the Icelandic Republic, with the flag and the four guardian spirits. He walked up the steps and was about to knock when he heard a voice call in Icelandic:

'Here, down here!'

The voice rose up a set of steep steps at the side of the front entrance. Peering over the black-painted handrail, Gunnar looked straight down the throat of a thin-haired man in a light-coloured moleskin jacket. He gestured to Gunnar to hurry up and come down to the basement.

Inside, there were storerooms and the office of the embassy caretaker. A row of cardboard boxes lined the corridor, with obsolete typewriters stacked on top. The walls were hung with faded colour photographs of Icelandic beauty spots. There was a wide-bellied vacuum cleaner lying on its side on the green felt carpet. In the coffee room, an electric kettle was boiling.

A soft hand darted from the sleeve of the man's jacket:

'Valur Sveinsson, commercial attaché in the posh quarters upstairs.'

'Gunnar Kampen, Pálsson.'

The commercial attaché spooned instant coffee into two mugs, then filled one and pushed it towards Gunnar. But Gunnar hastily declined, explaining that he was in a hurry as he had to make another call before he caught the morning train from Paddington to Cheltenham Spa. It was his first time travelling across London and he wanted to make sure he didn't miss it.

'You're going like that, are you?'

Valur Sveinsson pointed at the pyjama bottoms visible below his coat. Gunnar nodded and replied that he had almost overslept and rushed out just as he was. It wasn't true. Naturally, he had intended to get dressed but an emergency on the ward had deprived him of the chance. On his way out he had grabbed his leather shoes and overcoat – having already stuffed all his papers into the pockets the day before.

'Oh well, it won't be the first time an outfit like that has been seen on the streets of the capital.'

Valur laid an envelope on the table. Lifting the flap, he revealed two bundles of pound notes and tapped the thicker one:

'Our friend at the National Bank asked me to convert this into pounds sterling for you. It's pretty generous.'

He ran a fingertip down the side of the bundle underneath: 'And this is from well-wishers in Iceland.'

Gunnar was lucky enough to get a seat on the top floor of the double-decker bus that took him to Notting Hill. The further he got from Sloane Square, the rougher the surroundings became and the more citizens filled the pavements. The inhabitants were in summer mode.

From the bus stop it was only a short walk to the British Nazi HQ on Princedale Road. There he was received by two young men, John and Alistair, in full party uniform – grey shirts, black ties, leather straps worn diagonally across the chest, and red sunwheels on the upper left arm; one in black jodhpurs and jackboots, the other in shorts and hiking shoes – who told him that unfortunately the plan had changed and the group had gone to the camp by car during the night. It would have attracted the attention of the authorities if they had all piled onto the same train. They themselves had stayed behind to defend the headquarters in case of attack. He must have noticed the hordes of blacks and half-castes in the area.

Gunnar was overwhelmed by exhaustion. He pulled up a stool and sat down at the conference table. While he was recovering his strength, Alistair sketched a map of the route from Cheltenham Spa to Pinnock Cliffs. He drew an 'X' at the destination, but John went one better and amused himself by changing the X into a swastika with a red biro.

'But there may be someone there to collect you, after all. Poul Engelen and his men were asking after you yesterday. You'll recognise them by their black shirts.'

He stuck the biro in Gunnar's breast pocket.

Gunnar rose to his feet. The NSM headquarters was magnificent: pictures of Adolf Hitler and Rudolf Hess took pride of place over a podium decorated with a carved eagle. There were piles of leaflets and magazines on the tables and shelves, and posters bearing slogans that made no attempt to disguise their meaning, featuring caricatures of blacks and hook-noses with bags of money. A frisson of joy ran through him: this is what the Munich 'Brown House' must have been like in the twenties.

It was delightful to travel by train again, even if the English compartments weren't a patch on the German ones.

He rested his cheek against the cool glass of the window.

Soon now he would be reunited with his Flemish friend, would meet Savitri Devi and George Lincoln Rockwell – who the British government had designated *persona non grata*, unaware that he had already entered the country incognito – along with countless other ardent souls he had got to know through exchanges of letters in recent years. This weekend, the World Union of National Socialists would become a reality. The manifesto was ready after many months of correspondence across the Atlantic. His signature would be added to it on behalf of the Icelandic Sovereign Power Movement. And his personal contribution would be to bring the new organisation a gift of money – his life savings and more. This time the world would be theirs.

'Excuse me, sir, was there anything else?'

Gunnar looks up. The scar has vanished from his forehead. In the doorway of the compartment stands a man of uncertain origin, dressed in the uniform of a steward. He is holding a round metal tray. In the middle of the tray, on a white cardboard mat bearing the British Railways logo, is a glass like the ones they used to have at home on Mánavallagata when Gunnar was small. It is brimming with red milk.

xxiv

The policeman with the notebook closes it over the pencil and returns it to his breast pocket. He calls down the corridor to the railway guard:

'We're all finished here. You can move the train now.'

He goes over to the body and shuts the dead man's eyes and mouth.

The spectators on the platform retreat towards the station building as the train emits a whistle of steam and begins to move off slowly in the direction of the siding where an ambulance is waiting with open doors to transport the young man back to London, to one of the city mortuaries.

The curtain is drawn across the window of the compartment.

Afterword

FROM BLACK PASTELS TO RED MILK

While I was writing *Red Milk*, a peculiar incident in my childhood came back to me. I must have been eight years old at the time as it happened during the period when my mother and I lived with my grandmother. For our art classes at school, we pupils had all been asked to buy a set of oil pastels, which were made by the Japanese firm Sakura and came in an exotic box decorated with line drawings of cherry blossom and photos of Mount Fuji – quite a handsome object for young Icelanders to possess. The nature of the pastels themselves was new to me. Unlike the hard American Crayolas we mostly used for our colouring books, which required a great deal of pressing onto the pulpy paper to emulate the bright greens, blues, yellows, reds and blacks of the Looney Tunes cartoons we saw at Sunday matinees, they were soft on the page, while the colours they produced were rich, strong and altogether more rewarding. They smelt good too.

I was always alone at home after school as both my mother and grandmother worked, my mother as a bank clerk in the centre of town and my grandmother in one of the last dairies in Reykjavík, not far from the house where we lived. I had my own key and food was left for me in the fridge. Should I want for anything else I could pop out to the dairy. Most of the time I spent playing with friends or reading books, which at that stage in my life ranged from academic editions of Icelandic folk tales and Greco-Roman myths to *Bob Morane* adventure stories. Newspapers too: my grandmother subscribed to the socialist newspaper *Thjódviljinn* (The People's Will), my mother to the more centrist *Tíminn* (The Times).

On one of those afternoons alone, well fed on rice pudding from the fridge and doughnut twists from the old Mackintosh tin, I took my cherished box of Japanese oil pastels out of my school bag and selected the black one. Then evidently – I can't remember the deed itself, only its aftermath – I used the stick to draw swastikas in heavy black, perfectly filled-in lines on one sheet of paper after another, taken from the memo pad I had brought from its place by the telephone into the bedroom I shared with my mother and where I had my own writing desk in the corner. I must have drawn two dozen of them in several variations. Some were askew on the square paper, some aligned with the edges of it, some were inside a circle, others inside a thick frame. In my mind's eye I can see myself looking at the freshly created swastikas laid out neatly on the desk in front of me, illuminated by the light of the Luxo lamp, which bent over them like the brightly lit tip of a question mark.

Then the memory of the aftermath hits me. The acute panic I felt as I realised that I had done something terribly wrong, that I shouldn't have drawn those cursed, crooked crosses, still resonates in my body. I knew that the carefully drawn black swastikas would not only shock my mother and grandmother should they see them; they would also make them sad and worried about their perfect little Sigurjón indulging in such a dark and senseless activity.

I gathered up the drawings in a hurry and tried to think of a way to get rid of them. I couldn't simply throw them in the bin. Even if I tore them into shreds the keen eyes of my grandmother would notice and she would easily piece the evidence together. Hiding them in the drawer of my writing desk was too risky as well. My mother might look in there if she needed to borrow a pencil for her crossword. The clock ticked, my grandmother would be home soon and shortly after that my mother. No place seemed safe enough for my secret stash of Nazi symbols. In the end I wrapped them up in a small plastic bag – they were sticky and smelt sugary – and with much effort and engineering I just about managed to raise a corner of the heavy cupboard in the hallway by the half centimetre I needed to slip the bag under one of its flat wooden feet. I washed my hands, sniffing them to make sure soap had replaced pastel, and made sure to scrape the black slivers from underneath my otherwise heavily gnawed fingernails.

In the coming days I regularly checked on the contraband package, fearing the cupboard might have slid on the thick rug so the plastic would stick out along the edges of the foot, but even though it stayed in position I moved it to two other hiding places before finally getting rid of it. The solution was simple. I stole a box of matches from the kitchen and took the swastika pages out to the field by the Kleppur mental hospital. And there, sheltering by a large rock, I set the whole lot on fire. The paper burned quickly and the flames were tinged blue from the black oil pastel; the smoke had a whiff of burning rubber.

I can only speculate about what brought this episode on. By 1970 it had been twenty-five years since the end of WWII. The Nazis on television were invariably depicted as monsters and I had no direct relationship with anyone who had been on the side of Germany in the war. Quite the opposite: my family leaned to the centre and left. But there was an untold story hiding under the surface in the peaceful household of three, the story of a family member I vaguely knew about but had never met – my mother's father. Today my best guess is that the deep shame both my mother and grandmother felt because of him was something I had picked up subconsciously. My mother had been born out of wedlock in 1936 and had been brought up by her grandparents in the East Fjords – that I knew, as well as that I myself had been born out of wedlock and brought up with an absent father – while my grandmother moved to Reykjavík. There she married a fine man, who was a captain on the fishing boats and a committed socialist, and bore him three children before his untimely death twelve years before my birth.

None of this was a secret. But it was only when I became a teenager that it was revealed to me that my grandfather, who by then I had met once and found warm but aloof, had lived in Germany and come to Iceland on a U-boat in April 1944. When he and his companion reached shore on their inflatable dinghy they turned themselves in, but also admitted that they had been trained to spy for the Germans. After spending a year in prison in England he was handed over to the Icelandic authorities and convicted of treason, and although the twelve-month jail term was considered to have already been served, he was stripped of his right to vote or run for office. This was big news to me, since I had grown up with the notion that my family's history had not intersected with the war in any way. And as it linked myself to that great narrative by proxy, I believe it became an essential part of the self-image I was developing. I didn't feel any shame about it, instead it made me aware of how close we still were to the dark forces of the recent past, and I am sure it is why I have frequently been drawn to those in my writing.

It was much later that I came to understand how painful it must have been for my leftist grandmother to be so closely associated with a Nazi sympathiser. For that is what he was, along with his father and most of his brothers. As for my mother, she grew up knowing only that her father had been in the news when she was six years old, because of something so bad that no one in her small fishing village would tell her what it was. She was also in her teens when she finally learned the truth about what he had done. So maybe it was the sense of this unacknowledged disgrace, shared between mother and daughter, that got to me at eight and I reacted to it by instinctively drawing the evil symbol at the heart of it? Maybe.

* * *

Red Milk started taking shape in my mind when I reflected on how I had dealt with the presence of National Socialist ideals in Iceland in two of my earlier works, The Whispering Muse and CoDex 1962. In those novels I took an ironic stance towards the various characters' use of Nazism's racial ideas and obsession with Nordic culture to inflate their own importance in the world. And I treated their attitudes in the flippant manner that befitted my intended takedown of such elements in Icelandic society and self-identity. So, thinking about it again, I realised that I had still to explore the matter from a wholly serious point of view. That in a sense I 'owed' such a book to the victims of the ideology that I had until now satirised, and even had fun with in the case of *The Whispering Muse,* which was based on the laughable but unforgivable racial 'theories' of my great-grandfather, the father of a group of card-carrying Nazi brothers in the Westman Islands.

In my research for the earlier novels I had come across information about a small neo-Nazi group that operated in Reykjavík in the late '50s and early '60s. Not much was known about it and if it was written about at all it was usually brushed off as an aberration in our post-war history. But when I decided to take a closer look at the subject of National Socialism and Iceland it was this particular group that caught my writer's imagination, as there is always an opportunity for fiction in wilfully forgotten, repressed stories. And as my research uncovered the fact that one of the main actors within that small group had not only been in close contact with Savitri Devi, George Lincoln Rockwell, Colin Jordan and Göran Asser Oredsson – the very people who laid the foundation for the international network of far-right movements as we know it today – but had died from cancer at a young age while fanatically working on the foundation of their World Union of National Socialists, then I knew I had found a character who could carry that untold story. He had struggled for that abominable cause until his dying breath: now was the time for the autopsy.

Thus the character of Gunnar Kampen was born and the only way for me to write about him was to treat him, his ideas and the events of his life with the kind of humane respect he and his fellow travellers under the spell of Hitlerism, racism and white supremacy would never show their 'enemies': the Reds, the Fags, the Jews, the Blacks and others. But I have to admit that it was his early death, which I soon knew would be revealed on the novel's first page, that made it possible for me to write about how he came to be who he was at the end of his life in the clinical way I deemed necessary. And I suppose that by extension it makes it more acceptable to most readers to follow him on that journey, knowing that it will be cut short. It is easier to deal with a dead Nazi than a living one.

It has always served me well when writing my books to look for what I have in common with my characters, especially when it comes to the less appetising aspects of their personalities. But ironically, in the case of Gunnar Kampen I found that we shared something more appealing – a burning passion for an unpopular cause we believed was unjustly denied its role in transforming the world. Therefore much of the fervent activity that marked my days as a teenage surrealist from the late '70s to the mid '80s went into understanding how he operated his Nazi cell twenty years earlier. Both of us reached out to important people abroad in search of support for our little groups. I have mentioned the people contacted by the model for Gunnar Kampen. I myself wrote to every active surrealist who had had the misfortune of his or her address falling into my lap. With some I corresponded for years, while others never replied to the manifesto-riddled letters written to them in halting English by an eighteen-year-old in Reykjavík. I even went on a pilgrimage to France to meet members of André Breton's final circle and as a result was invited by his widow, the Chilean artist Elisa Breton, to stay with her for five days in their medieval summer house in Saint-Cirq-Lapopie. I returned to Iceland, fully alive after having been baptised into Surrealism by a dragonfly while swimming in the river Lot.

When I'm planning a new novel, I invariably begin by deciding what not to do as much as what needs to be done to create the book I'm aiming for. With *The Blue Fox* I decided against ever depicting the inner life of Abba, the young woman with Down's syndrome; with *From The Mouth Of The Whale* I decided I couldn't tell the story of its seventeenth-century protagonist in a third-person narrative related by a man from the future, and that it had to take place inside the character's own pre-Enlightenment mind as much as possible; with *Moonstone: The Boy Who Never Was* I decided I must not show any sympathy for the lovely, queer, imaginative, sixteen-year-old cinephile Máni Steinn – he had to survive on his own and should he gain the reader's goodwill, he had to have earned it himself.

With *Red Milk*, what I wouldn't allow myself to do was employ pathos or myth. I decided that in the story there would be no epiphanies, no dreams, no moments of agony, nor would there be a fervent engagement with the Nordic pantheon or its symbols, or any feeding off the heroic deeds and words of the characters from the Icelandic sagas. There are hints of all of this in Gunnar Kampen's world, that is for sure, but as the neo-Nazis' own narratives are driven so much by an emotional connection with these elements, in the hope of attaining or confirming their superiority, I had to refrain from using them. Everything that ultimately serves to make Nazism exotic had to be put aside. What I was looking for instead was what made my character normal to the point of banality.

That is to say, in order to begin to understand what makes it possible for people to heed the call of Nazism in all its guises, old and new – identitarian, alt-right, True or National this and that – after the devastation wrought by Adolf Hitler and his gang of criminals and after what is possibly the best-documented premeditated genocide in history, the Holocaust, we must start with what we have in common with such people. Not that I think a proper conversation can ever be had with someone whose ultimate goal is to get rid of you for good. But we can at least show them that we see them for what they are, that we know they come from childhoods fundamentally similar to our own, that had they been nudged in a different direction by individuals and events at the beginning of their journeys, they could so easily have become something else – that a neo-Nazi is no more special than that.

Acknowledgements

p. 3: Quotation from the English translation of *Also Sprach Zarathustra* by Friedrich Nietzsche, taken from p. 137 of *The Portable Nietzsche*, edited and translated by Walter Kaufmann, published by The Viking Press, New York, 1954.

p. 10: This stanza is an adaptation of *Ásukvæði*, recorded by Bjarni Þorsteinsson in *Íslensk þjóðlög*, published in Copenhagen, 1909.

p. 46: Quotation from the poem *Í Babýlon við Faxafjörð* by Rev. Björn Halldórsson from Laufás.

p. 58: Excerpt from pp. 96–7 of *Akhnaton: A Play* by Savitri Devi Mukherji, published by The Philosophical Publishing House, London, 1948.

p. 63: *The Prose Edda*, our best source for Old Norse mythology, is a handbook on poetics, written in thirteenth-century Iceland and attributed to Snorri Sturluson (1179–1241).

pp. 91–5: The text of *New Mjölnir* is adapted from the first issue of *Frjáls Evrópa*, published by the Nordic Realm Party in Iceland, 1961.

p. 110: Extract from *Under Milk Wood* by Dylan Thomas, first performed in New York, 1953.

Thanks are due to Una Margrét Jónsdóttir and Þórarinn Eldjárn for their help in finding derogatory verses about Reykjavík, and to Roy Jacobsen for his assistance in deciding the fate of a Norwegian quisling.

SJÓN

The Blue Fox

Winner of the Nordic Council Literature Prize

On a stark Icelandic mountainside, the imposing Reverend Baldur Skuggason hunts an elusive blue vixen for her near-mythical pelt. The treacherous journey across snow and ice will push his physical and mental endurance to the limit.

In Baldur Skuggason's parish, a young woman with Down's Syndrome is buried. After being found shackled to the timbers of a shipwreck in 1868, she was rescued by the naturalist Fridrik B. Fridjonsson. Now he will open the package she always carried with her, hoping to solve the puzzle of her origins.

As the ice begins to melt, the mystery surrounding the trio's connected fates is unravelled in this spellbinding fable, an exquisite tale of metamorphosis.

'Enchantingly poetic . . . spellbinding . . .
magical . . . exceptional'
Independent

'A magical novel'
Björk

'Describes its world with brilliant, precise, concrete colour
and detail . . . Comic and lyrical.'
AS Byatt, *The Times*

'A taut, poetic and beautifully judged fable'
Times Literary Supplement

'Wondrous . . . with a strange black humour at its core.'
Dazed & Confused

SCEPTRE

SJÓN

The Whispering Muse

Winner of the Icelandic Bookseller's Prize for
Novel of the Year

Valdimar Haraldsson is an eccentric Icelander with dubious
ideas about the relationship between fish consumption and
Nordic superiority. To his delight, in the spring of 1949, he
is invited to join a Danish merchant ship on its voyage to
the Black Sea.

He is less delighted with the lack of fish on the menu.
Worse, his fellow travellers show no interest in his 'Fish and
Culture' lecture. They prefer the enthralling tales of the
second mate, Caeneus, who every evening regales them with
his adventures aboard the Argo, on Jason's legendary quest
for the Golden Fleece.

Sjón weaves together Greek and Nordic myths with the lega-
cies of the Second World War in this mesmerising novel,
which reminds us that everything is capable of change.

'A quirky, melodic, ticklish, seamlessly translated, lovingly
polished gem of a novel.'
David Mitchell

'Funny, strange, provoking and disturbing; darkness
with a light touch.'
Times Literary Supplement

'Sjón pulls off the difficult task of creating an unboring bore with
panache. Not only that, he allows a twist at the end that changes
our perspective . . . He has changed the way I see things.'
AS Byatt, *New York Review of Books*

'Sublime . . . A work of coy humor and shape-shifting magic.'
Wall Street Journal

SCEPTR

SJÓN

From the Mouth of the Whale

Shortlisted for the *Independent* Foreign Fiction Prize and
the International IMPAC Dublin Literary Award

In this magical evocation of a vanished age, a poet and
self-taught healer is banished in 1635 to a barren island
off Iceland – a place darkened by superstition,
poverty and cruelty.

With only a purple sandpiper for company, Jónas Pálmason
retraces his path to exile, recalling his exorcism of a walking
corpse, the massacre of innocent Basque whalers at
the hands of local villagers and the deaths of three
of his children.

But amid the cacophony of Copenhagen he will find hope
and, finally, recognition of his enlightened ideas.
'Hallucinatory, lyrical, by turns comic and tragic . . .
extraordinary.'
Hari Kunzru

'A terrific read . . . an extraordinarily accomplished novel'
Independent

'Kaleidoscopic and mesmerising, comic and poignant'
Times Literary Supplement

'Strange and wonderful'
Junot Díaz

'Wildly comic and incandescent, elegant and brittle.'
Washington Post

SCEPTRE

SJÓN

Moonstone: The Boy Who Never Was

Winner of the Icelandic Literary Award

In October 1918, the Katla volcano erupts, colouring the skies over Reykjavík night and day. Yet life in the small capital carries on as usual, with the Great War grinding distantly on. Then the Spanish flu comes ashore, killing hundreds and driving thousands to their sick beds. The streets empty, the cinemas close and for sixteen-year-old Máni Steinn – a film fanatic and dreamer who hovers on the fringes of society – everything changes. Capturing Iceland at a moment of profound transformation, this is the story of a misfit in a place where life and death, reality and imagination, secrets and revelations jostle for dominance.

'Sjón's slim, simmering masterpiece . . . a pitch-perfect study of transgression, survival and love'
David Mitchell

'A work of miniaturist perfection: a brief, brilliant jewel of a book'
Guardian

'A magical book, the work of a great illusionist . . . unforgettable'
Adam Foulds

'Eerie and enchanted'
The Economist, 1843

'Emotion never gets lost in the intricacies of his storytelling . . . a small book with a huge heart.'
New Statesman

'A deeply felt novel . . . sure to delight his fans and convert many new ones'
Hari Kunzru, *Guardian*

SCEPTRE

SJÓN

CoDex 1962

Winner of the *DV* Newspaper Culture Prize / Literature

Jósef Loewe claims to remember the moment of his birth on a kitchen table in Reykjavík in 1962. But he also traces his origins back to Germany at the height of the Second World War and to a lump of clay, shaped into a baby by his fugitive Jewish father . . .

Truth, dreams, fantasies and fable coalesce in the captivating story of Jósef's life and times, the narrative of a man trying to make sense of the modern world and his place in it. Spanning continents, eras and genres, this is a boundary-breaking, electrifying novel by an Icelandic master.

'A work of virtuoso narrative . . . an Icelandic *1001 Nights*'
Sunday Times

'A raconteur of talent. He can flick from angelic frolics to seedy violence as if each tale were a smooth refraction of the last. He has a knack for high comedy, too.'
Daily Telegraph

'An extraordinary performance . . . the effect is hypnotic
. . . His wild, subversive imagination is among his great strengths, not only *in CoDex 1962* but throughout his work.'
Guardian

'Bewitching'
The Economist

'I can only echo Loewe, with gratitude, exasperation and awe: "This book's a bloody thief of time."'
New York Times

SCEPTRE

NICOLAS MATHIEU

And Their Children After Them

Winner of the Prix Goncourt

August 1992. Fourteen-year-old Anthony and his cousin
decide to steal a canoe to fight their all-consuming
boredom on a lazy summer afternoon. Their simple act
of defiance will lead to Anthony's first love and his first
real summer – that one summer that comes to define
everything that follows.

Over four sultry summers in the 1990s, Anthony and his
friends grow up in a gritty France trapped between nostalgia
and decline, decency and rage, desperate to escape their
small town, the scarred countryside and grey council estates
in search of a more hopeful future.

'A page-turner of a novel'
New York Times Book Review

'An exceptional portrait of youth, ennui and class divide'
John Boyne, *Irish Times*

'A lyrical, almost-Lawrentian saga of left-behind France'
Boyd Tonkin, *Spectator* Books of the Year

'Masterly'
Times Literary Supplement

'An elegiac anthem'

Financial Times

SCEPTR

MIROSLAV PENKOV

Stork Mountain

Into a remote corner of Bulgaria comes an American
student, returning to his native country to track down his
grandfather, who inexplicably cut off all contact with the
family three years earlier.

The trail ends in a mountain village on the border with
Turkey, a stone's throw away from Greece – a place of pagan
mysteries and ancient feuds, where religious fault lines run
deep. Here he is led by his grandfather into a maze of
half-truths, and falls in love with an unobtainable Muslim
girl. Old ghosts come back to life and forgotten conflicts
blaze anew before the past finally yields up its secrets.

'Gorgeous and big-hearted . . . a fantastic book'
Molly Antopol

'A historically rich study of borders: those imposed by
cartography and those that are self-constructed.'
Financial Times

'A dark, dreamlike debut novel steeped in Balkan history
and legend . . . beautiful and haunting.'
Chicago Review of Books

'Wildly ambitious . . . thoughtful and thought-provoking,
with a passionate faith in the redemptive powers of art.'
Boston Globe

SCEPTRE

Join a literary community of
like-minded readers who seek out
the best in contemporary writing.

From the thousands of submissions Sceptre
receives each year, our editors select the books
we consider to be outstanding.

We look for distinctive voices, thought-provoking
themes, original ideas, absorbing narratives and
writing of prize-winning quality.

If you want to be the first to hear about our
new discoveries, and would like the chance to
receive advance reading copies of our books
before they are published, visit

www.sceptrebooks.co.uk

 Follow @sceptrebooks

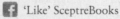 'Like' SceptreBooks

 Watch SceptreBooks